The Human Season

Edward Lewis Wallant

THE HUMAN SEASON

Harbrace Paperbound Library
Harcourt Brace Jovanovich, Inc.
New York

© 1960 by Edward Lewis Wallant
ISBN 0-15-642330-8
Library of Congress Catalog Card Number: 60-10923
Printed in the United States of America
A B C D E F G H I J

The Human Season

Berman sat alone now on his sofa. For just a minute or two he felt relief at the silence. But then the quiet became dark and threatening like a vessel filling with a strange liquid.

"Well," he said. His voice shocked him, spilled the silence on him so he had to get up hurriedly and touch something.

He touched the couch fabric, smoothed the velvet-like nap so all the texture ran the right way. That always bothered her, he thought, to see the hairs going the wrong way on the couch.

He straightened suddenly as though to be on guard against someone who might come from behind him. Of course there was no one. . . .

"I'll make some tea . . . tea."

He was a big, heavy man and the old floors creaked under him even beneath the moss-green carpeting. The glasses and little antique cups he had always ridiculed her for buying ("So little, you could only get a mouthful of coffee out of them") rattled delicately in the colonial corner cupboards in the dining room. "Demi-tiss," he said in a croaking voice as he hurried almost fearfully by them.

The kitchen was large and square and painted carefully in a

9

color the painter had insisted was "A leetle bit off-white." It had been a joke between them. "A leetle bit off-white," he would say and she would smile and wave away his foolishness.

He went to the sink and ran the water. As he stood there the plant on one of the little knickknack shelves tickled his nose with a light, feminine touch. He jerked his head up in shock to stare at the shiny leaves. Suddenly his eyes widened. He seized the little flowerpot painted lovingly with his wife's idea of forget-me-nots. For a moment he held it in a wild, raging uncertainty. Then he dashed it to the floor, where it smashed and left a scattering of soil and greenery on the maroon linoleum.

As he stared down at the destruction, the phone rang. He lurched toward it desperately as though one more ring would destroy him.

"Yes, yes," he roared into the mouthpiece.

"Daddy," his daughter said into his ear.

"Yeh." His face underwent a crafty concealment as though she could see him.

"Are you all right?" she asked.

"You just left me twenny minutes . . . how should I be?"

"No, I mean I was thinking all the way home about you being alone there. I don't feel right."

"Let's not go all over that," Berman said. He studied the shiny scar tissue over his amputated index finger. He had such thick hands, plumber's hands.

"No, I mean it, Daddy. It's so soon after Mother passing . . ." Her voice caught in a little bubble of grief. "It's so soon for you to be all alone so suddenly."

"You stayed here a month. It's enough. Your husband and your children need you," he said in his rough voice. Unaccountably he remembered how his daughter had looked at nine —dark-skinned, thin, homely. He could never have foreseen that some man would want to marry her, would hunger after her as he had hungered for her mother. . . .

"Yes, but you could come to stay with us, live with us instead of staying there all alone. You know there's plenty of room. The children would be so happy to have you here."

"Look, we went all over it a dozen times." His voice was not gentle or affectionate. There was no way to tell by his voice how much Berman loved. "I'll say it again. I want to try it by myself for a while, at least give it six months, to see. . . ."

"But *why,* Daddy, why must you?"

Her voice, reduced by the telephone, was like a memory in his ear. He had never liked talking on the telephone, always had felt the possibility of it all being a joke, a toy voice. Face to face was the way he liked to talk.

"Look, it's a terrible thing He did to me, God. I'm not goin' into it any more now. But it caught me in the middle. . . . I'm fifty-nine. All right, if I was ten years younger there might be some kind of a life to start again. And if I was ten years older I could get myself used to bein' the old grandpa, living in my children's house, quiet, out of the way, helping a little, you know . . . like old people. But I'm in the middle, see, halfway. So I got to try and figure out for myself."

"Oh, Daddy," she wailed into his ear, defeated for now.

"Don't worry, don't worry. I'll be all right." Then he hung up as he always did, without saying good-by, for he was impatient with the little meaningless amenities.

He got up and went to the broom closet for the dustpan and mop. Her aprons hung there, faded and thin and soft against his horny, thick hands.

Carefully he swept the pieces of flowerpot, the crumbs of dirt into the dustpan. He dumped the debris into the paper bag in the wastebasket. Then he hung the pan and brush back in the little broom closet beside the aprons.

He put the kettle on to boil and sat down to wait for it. He brushed at some microscopic crumbs on the table's oilcloth, fussed at the frayed edge for a moment until he recognized the gesture with horror as not being his own.

He got up and looked out the window. The next house was only about fifteen feet away. The white siding was overlaid with about five years' accumulation of soot. To the left, past a sloppily installed leader (not like he would have done it), he could see his neighbor's long, narrow yard with its one frayed-looking cherry tree. The man was a fool, he thought, out there every night with his gardening cap on, spraying the patchy, miserable grass, forever puttering with the tiny squares of dirt in front which stubbornly refused to grow even weeds. No, that nonsense was not for him. Give him a fifty by a hundred of good, clean cement. These putterers, these after-hours artisans. If they had *worked* as *he* had worked in his life . . .

And then the tea was done so he could pour it into the glass and get the cube sugar and drink it, feeling a mild stir of satisfaction at how he had conquered a whole five minutes.

Afterwards he washed the glass very thoroughly and dried it till it gleamed. Then he put it up with the other glasses of all shapes and sizes, some of which had been jelly jars, some of which had contained the wax for the memorial candles he and Mary had lit for their parents at different times of the year for as long as they had been married. His mother was in the Hebrew month of Heshvan and her mother had died in Tebet.

He slammed the cupboard door shut, winced at the brutal loudness of the sound, then touched lightly and almost apologetically at the knob, which had a strange warmth for metal, as though someone had held a hand against it, transmitting the body heat for a long time.

From the middle of the large, gleaming kitchen he surveyed

the possible directions he could take. The refrigerator hummed its cool efficiency and the pilot light of the stove was a small blue eye in the growing dimness. He went to the wall switch, which had a flowered plate over it, and switched on the light. And standing there in all the chrome and formica and gleaming enamel, he created a moment of spiteful pleasure for himself.

"Buttons, switches—I'm a magician."

He clicked the light off and went down the long hall that led to the bathroom.

The bathroom had a silent switch and the fluorescent lights came out of the darkness like artificial sunlight escaping a cloud. Everything was tile and mirror in there. The toilet was of the latest design, longer and lower and gracefully curved. His grin was brutal as he began to urinate into it, grew harsher as he scorned his old delicacy, which had made him aim the stream at the edges of the toilet where it made no sound. Now he made a vulgar splash in the center of the water and the smile went even worse, became a grimace as the periodic pain from his surgically shrunken bladder seized him. "'Agghhhh-hhh . . .'"

His face was on two sides of him. The larger mirror, over the double sink, had a rose tint to it. His face stared back at him as through a thin solution of blood, big-nosed, furrowed, spectacled in fashionable horn rims. He was bald on top, gray-ing on the sides. His green sport shirt cast some of its color up onto his face, which in the rosy glass took on a putty color. Such an ugly face, he thought. How had it ever been loved?

Distastefully he shrugged at the face and the whole gleaming room of faucets and switches and mirrors. On a little glass shelf stood the soft pastel colors of lotions and shampoos. There still seemed to be a clinging scent of powder, a rustling feminine fragrance. He began to tremble a little there in that hard, shining chamber. Silkiness obsessed him suddenly and he ran his hands stiff-fingered down the glossy shower curtain so the tiny threads snagged against his roughened fingertips with a miniature ripping sound.

He switched off the silent light and walked more heavily than necessary, taking a brief comfort in the sound of the floor yielding to his weight and the rooms carrying at least that human note through themselves. Past the bedroom that had been his daughters', with the modern, solid-maple twin beds; past his son's room, a sort of spare-room catchall for the past thirteen years, with mothproof garment bags and an ironing board, the typewriter his wife had used to make out bills, suitcases and hat boxes—and, indeed, nothing of his son except a poorly enlarged, grainy photograph which showed the boy holding a ridiculously small fish and wearing a sweat shirt that said A.Z.A. on the front, and a pennant that said Hillhouse in white flannel letters on faded blue. So past his own bedroom, with the big, heavily carved double bed, which had a deep hollow in the center as though only one heavy body had lain there all those years. Then through the kitchen again and the dining room, until he was in the living room at the front of the house and could go no farther.

There was a mirror in the living room, too, over the sealed-off fireplace with its neat stack of white-birch logs that would never know fire. The big-nosed, grooved face looked back at him bewilderedly, and he thought of the old ritual of covering the mirrors in time of mourning. He had come a long way from the old rituals, although he still practiced most of the important precepts. She used to scold him teasingly for wearing his hat in the house, and although he used to claim he had just forgotten to take it off, both of them knew that instinctive gesture of respect for God was buried in his forgetfulness, so they never pursued it too far.

Berman began swiveling his head from side to side, pretending to himself he was looking for some tangible object. Really, though, he was gasping through the dying light, drowning in the dimming, echoless emptiness of the house. His hands fluttered at his sides, his head turned from right to left, and as he swayed in peculiar vertigo, he wondered, if he should fall, whether he would land on solid floor or keep falling through the endless dimness that sucked color and shape from all the furniture and walls he thought he had known so well.

"All right, all right, I'm a magician, I can push switches. . . . Why do I stand in the dark?" With something like courage he forced himself over to the lamp and switched on the light. The room leaped out in nightmare reality. The same room, nothing changed. Except everything. Tears leaked feebly from the corners of his eyes like matter from a wound he wasn't concerned with. "It's silly," he said. "I'm tired is what I am. The sleeping pills give me sleep without rest. I'm tired enough, I won't take them; I don't need them any more."

He felt stimulated at the thought of all the preparations for bed, definite things to do. He went into the kitchen and took the bag of rubbish from the pail. Then he carried it down the long hall to the back door and out to the yard. There was a moon in the sky, hazy and threatening, less bright than all the back windows of the houses. The clothesline creaked faintly in a light breeze and a house dress moved gently on its clothespins, inhabited by the phantom night air. Berman walked down the little flagstone path to the burner and dropped the bag in. He considered burning it but found he had no matches with him. There was a smell of ashes and moist ground. The scrubby grass seemed to roll at his feet like the rippled surface of water. He took a deep breath and held it for a moment, considered the possibility of holding it forever, then exhaled, with the defeated sound of derision making a puffing noise from his heavy lower lip. He wished there were something he had to take into the house. The house dress swayed before him, blocking out the ugly moon. He reached up for it but its worn softness repelled him, so he left it there in the summer night and walked back into the house.

In the bathroom he went through the slight pain of elimination, this time urinating carefully on the side of the toilet as though following some rule he had reaffirmed for the while. He even brushed his scattered brown teeth; this was something he had done only sporadically, in spite of Mary's years of urging. Then he washed thoroughly with soap and washcloth and handbrush. It was one thing he was very conscientious about, as soon as he came in the back door from work each night. He would greet no one, touch no one until he was scrubbed clean and changed from the greasy clothes. His wife had been so proud of his fanatic love of cleanliness, used to boast of it to other people, saying, "Oh, my Joe may clean toilet waste all day but he comes to me white as snow. . . ."

He went into the bedroom and hung up his clothes. He never wore pajamas, slept instead in his underwear. His wife had stopped teasing him about it years before. His cleanness made up to her for a lot of little things. He used to tell her he didn't like to make such a big thing of sleep, dressing specially for it. Anyhow, he liked to put on his pants the moment he set foot to the floor, like putting on his man's responsibilities and dignity.

"No sleeping pills," he reminded himself defiantly.

He lay down stiffly on the bed. It felt damp, and haunted with lumps he had never noticed before. His body stayed rigid and an unbearable fatigue filled him.

"Ah, this is no good," he said, sitting up. He got up and put his pants on. Then, taking the pillow under his arm, he padded barefoot to the living room and arranged the pillow on the sofa. With a great sigh he laid himself down. He repeated the sigh and forced a yawn as though he would convince himself he was ready for sleep.

But his eyes were held open by an invisible stiffness and he lay watching the pattern of the street lights cut up and moved by the slow-moving branches of the maple tree in front of the house. A car's headlights swept the blinds. Then a woman's heels clicked by on the sidewalk.

Slowly, almost fastidiously, he began in a low, hoarse voice to curse God, made it more personal and sincere by uttering his curses in Yiddish there in the carpeted, dusty, muffling room.

April 30, 1956

To Berman Friday evening held the most precious hours of the week. Maybe Mary liked the Saturday card games; sure, he did, too. But Friday . . .

Little remained of their Sabbath rituals, the special dinners they used to have in the beginning. She lit the candles, it was true. But their suppers were for just the two of them and were likely to consist of tuna-fish salad or bologna sandwiches and coffee. The old ritual had been replaced by something easier and more intimate. The daughters had gone their ways, the son was gone forever, and there was time to talk of little things, make little comforting complaints in the bright, labor-saving kitchen, exchange bits of gossip, and assay their situation as to finances and obligations. They decided that evening, as they sat there—Mary with her big, blue child's eyes, slightly goiterous in her still pretty face, he sipping gingerly at the coffee scalding hot as he liked it—that they would give each of their married daughters a five-hundred-dollar check.

"Now, when they can use it," Berman said.

"She needs a rug, Ruthie," Mary said, never able to stay on the big schemes of her husband, always having to pin it down to some tangible item.

"The way I see it . . ." Berman went on, comfortable in the presence of that particular face, for which all his discourses were created. All day, half-consciously, he wove his thoughts

as he worked, finally bringing to her at the supper table the
homely yet substantial fabric that made a design of their days.
". . . in three years the mortgage is payed off, right?"

Her nod pushed him on. She gazed tiredly over his shoulder.
That was the way she listened, as though it gave her leeway to
jump off his conversation from time to time, to perch on some
little thought of her own for a moment before returning to him.

"Okay, then I take a second mortgage out and do the whole
house over, top to bottom. Then we're set, see. And *then* . . ."
He looked slyly at her, waiting for her to look curiously at him,
which she finally did.

"All right, Joe, don't make a big mystery. Say it."

"Then the real idea . . ."

"Oh, how you like to drag out a story. Tell it, already, before I get up and do the dishes." Mild exasperation showed on
her delicately lined face. She had many wrinkles, but thin,
shallow ones, which Berman thought beautiful. She had had
them since she was much younger, when she had been very
sick.

"It's all right. I'll tell you while we do the dishes."

She stood facing the sink, washing; he stood drying with his
back to her. The refrigerator hummed, the water sloshed
peacefully in the sink. Outside there was a lonely wind.

"Well, I figure we'll just take ourselfs a little trip out to
California to see Debby."

"Joe, you're crazy. Do you know what that would cost! Besides, she comes here every three months to visit."

"Listen to the woman—no sense at all. Never mind her this
time. This time I'm not thinking of the children. Us, we're the
ones. It's time for us to live a little."

"But, Joe . . ."

"It's no use. I've made up my mind."

"Do you have any idea the clothes I'll need. All I have is
. . ."

Berman began to laugh, recognizing her focusing down to tangibles as acquiescence. He spun a plate up in the air, delighting in her shocked inhalation.

"Joe, have you gone out of your mind?"

"Sure," he said merrily, and began putting the dried dishes up into the cupboard, smiling all the while, enjoying her disapproving head shaking over her own smile.

Then later they sat and watched television, and, by rote, he made sardonic observations on the unrealities of the plays while she, intent on what took place on the black-and-white stage, waved his sarcasms off impatiently as though they could impede her projection into the stories.

At about ten o'clock, she went into the bedroom to read the paper, and he watched the fights. There was a certain warmth in being off in a male appreciation, knowing his woman was in his bed, protected by walls he had created, safe, abiding. Then, somewhere in the middle of the fight, during a commercial, he went into the bedroom and took her glasses off her sleeping eyes, removed the paper from her body, and went back to the fight.

At eleven o'clock, he made a pot of coffee and rattled the cups with unnecessary noise so she would wake and say what she always said.

"Oh, Joe, the coffee smells delicious."

And he didn't smile with his mouth, for his pleasure was very old now, but he smiled in his heart without thinking about it.

They sat and talked some more over coffee and odds and ends of food—pieces of cheese, the remains of a can of sardines, cake, cold meat.

Berman took the dishes to the sink as he talked. He washed the cups and saucers, the small plates (the ones with sardine oil carefully with cold water first). And then, after a while, he remarked at her unusual silence and turned to see her sitting a little bewildered, pointing at her throat.

"What's the matter, swallow something?" he asked.

She shook her head and indicated she couldn't talk.

"Laryngitis," he decreed, feeling only the slightest unease. "Berman will fix you up." He went to the refrigerator and got out the Alka-Seltzer. Everything was so easy nowadays. You didn't need to depend so much on Providence as in the old days. "Okay, take this," he said, handing her the fizzing liquid, "and then go right to bed. Skip the bath for once."

She nodded with unusual docility and went into the bedroom. For a moment he looked after her with a frown, then shrugged it away and returned to the living room to watch a late movie.

Much later, he went back to the bedroom. She was sleeping peacefully, though breathing a little more heavily than usual. Her mouth was open. Sometimes she slept that way when she was overtired. He lay down, but some unfathomable alertness refused to let his eyes close. He got up on one elbow to watch her. Her face was very white in the pale haze of moonlight, which came indirectly, reflected from the white house next door into their room. The wrinkles were invisible and she was white. Her body was white, always had been white and soft and un-utterably clean, so clean. . . . After a while his elbow, his whole arm, became stiff, so he got out of bed and sat in the little boudoir chair, his eyes constant on her sleeping face. Was her breathing strange? He looked for evidence to trigger real alarm, to give him motive for doing something. Her breathing sounded peculiarly hoarse, but regular, strong. His imagination, but still . . . He tried to invent excuses for waking her, for positive fear, but all he felt was a strange, chilling melancholy. And he watched her like that, teetering the whole night through over a depth of something terrifying, seeing her young in the moonlight, then finally aging in the gray of dawn, more and more until the first sunlight showed her older than he had realized and he got up and shook her awake.

Her eyes opened; she smiled. For a minute gladness covered him like the sun's warmth. Then he noticed the clouded bewilderment in her eyes.

"How do you feel?" he asked.

She shrugged and pushed her feet off the bed.

"Can you talk yet?"

She shook her head. She still seemed very sleepy.

"Do you want me to help you?" he asked, reaching out his hand as she stood up.

She pushed past him, went out into the hall and down toward the bathroom. Berman followed, noticing with an icy despair how she dragged one foot so she had to hold the wall.

He stood in the bathroom doorway, watching her before the big, rose-colored mirror. She began combing her hair, which was gray, but thick and wavy like a mane. Her strokes were wooden, automatic, like something remembered. She picked up some bobby pins. She couldn't find her head, made stabbing, wild motions in the air with the little black pins. Finally she jammed one into her nose, gave a gasp, and turned to him with terrible resignation on her face.

"What . . . what is it, Mary?" Berman cried.

And she just shook her head as though she could no longer fight against whatever it was happening to her. She staggered across the floor to him and threw her arms around his neck. They stood like that for some time and then Berman led her gently to the bed and called the doctor.

All that day he watched her in a hospital bed, with his daughter and son-in-law beside him. His younger daughter had been informed and was flying in from California.

At various times he noticed that her breathing got clogged, and he went out and called the always available doctor. At eight o'clock that night, although no one else noticed, Berman suddenly felt his wife leave him.

"She's gone," he told his daughter and the doctor. The doctor hurried into the room and Berman called after him, "Don't hurry, she's gone, she's gone, she's left me. . . ."

To his daughters' tears and consolations he had only one answer.

"I prayed, all my life I prayed. There, that's the good of it. . . ." And later he began to cry furiously, ferociously, so no one could get near him, and he kept crying that way for almost all of the next eighteen days.

CHAPTER TWO

He guessed he hadn't slept at all, for his eyes were dry and grainy in their sockets. The walls rose up around him, mocking with their rosebuds and gray leaves. The ceiling was a peculiar, arid terrain, crisscrossed by fine cracks like dry riverbeds. He had never realized how bad the ceilings were.

In the kitchen he started to get the coffeepot out, held it in his hand for a moment, gazing at the yellow sunlight on the floor. Then he put it back in the cupboard and took out a little saucepan instead. Far back on the shelf he found a half-jar of instant coffee. He put a half-teaspoonful into a large cup and when the water was hot, poured it into the cup. It tasted like dirty water, so he dumped it into the sink with a hiss of hatred.

He had just got his shirt on when he heard the familiar raucous groan of his partner's truck horn.

"I'm coming, I'm coming," he said. By instinct he went to the bedroom doorway. But then he realized there was nothing he wanted there so he hurried out the back door. He hung the key under the washtub over the cellar steps and wondered why he bothered now.

"Let them steal everything," he muttered. Then he felt dis-

23

gust with his childish petulance, for he meant much worse than petulance.

"Hullo, Yussel," his partner, Riebold, said, with pity rounding his big animal eyes. "I didn't know if you would be up to working yet. But I says to myself, it's the best thing for him, to get busy, take his mind off. Then I figure, the kids left yesterday so he's alone. Definite, absolutely definite he should get out and do a little work, take his mind off. . . ."

"All right, all right," Berman said impatiently as he climbed into the seat beside his partner. The familiar smell of greasy iron came from the back of the truck and the bucket seat was comfortingly hard and upright.

"Besides, I says to myself, it ain't so easy to go a month without work when you got all the—you know—expenses. . . ." He looked cautiously out of the corner of his eye at Berman, who sat silent, staring through the grimy windshield as though it were really opaque. "How 'bout if we stop for coffee?"

Berman shrugged.

Riebold gave a sigh at the towering job of communication he saw before him. He was a very poor driver, overcautious and slow. Once he had got a ticket for holding up traffic by going down the Boulevard, which was a fast-moving road, at only ten miles an hour. He stopped at every corner even when he had the right of way.

"It's a good job," he offered timidly. "Ryan's six-family on Grand Avenue, all new water pipes. Good for twelve hundred. I estimated twelve hundred but—you know—I like it better when you do the estimating."

"We'll see," Berman said gently, suddenly realizing he had no desire to hurt Riebold. "I'll take a look."

Riebold sighed again as he began slowing up for the corner a half-block away.

The cellar was ancient. Filth covered every stanchion and wall like thick paint. Small puddles of stagnant water shone with dull darkness in the feeble light from the high, dirty windows. Every time he moved, Berman felt the little wisps of spider web brush his face and the smell of urine and feces was very strong around where he was working. But his revulsion was so old and habitual that he was hardly conscious of it, and worked expressionlessly to the sound of footsteps on the floor over his head.

The old pipes were rust-welded together and he strained at the handle of the big Stillson wrench. The sweat chilled on him in that dank atmosphere as he struggled with the cold iron. He worked in little pockets of time, the few seconds closing around past and future constantly. It was hard for him even to think about the immediate motives for the particular thing he was doing. He knew only that he was pulling in a particular direction; when the pipe began to give, he would consider the next step. A rat suddenly ran over his ankle, splashed through one of the many puddles, then stopped to peer at him with polished eyes.

"Filth," he snarled, and fumbled around him for something to throw. But everything in reach was insubstantial, and in sudden, desperate rage, he pulled the wrench off the pipe and swung it savagely at the upright rat. The splash was muffled by the soft, crushed body. He pushed it away with the head of the wrench and turned back to the pipe. "Filthy shitten crap," he moaned. He threw a wild strength into his efforts and the pipe gave under the wrench.

"You get it?" Riebold called gaily as he came down the steps with a long piece of pipe over his powerful shoulder.

"I got it," Berman said tonelessly.

"A bitch, hah?"

"Rusted solid—you know. . . ."

"You gonna need a T?" Riebold asked, studying the results of Berman's work.

"Down here only a elbow, farther up the T . . ."

The technical talk of the work soothed him. Each problem had its solution in hard, unyielding metal. As much as he had always hated his work, he had felt a certain pleasant assuredness about it. He *knew* it, it held no mysteries for him, and for that alone it had been tolerable.

Later, Berman worked the pipe cutter in the yard while Riebold ate his lunch. Berman never ate lunch, never took a drink during the working day. He claimed food only made him drowsy at midday, and water, once started, became an obsession. More, perhaps, he felt a sort of chaste strength in not giving in to his body while he worked.

The sun was hot and made tiny shadows at the base of all the flotsam of the littered yard. Bits of glass winked in the sunlight. The pipe was almost hot to the touch. Berman noticed he cast a peculiar shadow, wedded to the shadow of the pipe-cutter, like a big, patient insect making a steady motion over his work. One of the tenants of the huge, shabby building, a massive colored woman, looked down sleepily from the second-floor porch. Berman worked, opening and closing the little patches of time, allowing only the immediate seconds to intrude on his consciousness.

He was just finishing the work in the cellar when a patch of bright yellow-orange jumped to the wall beside him. He gasped at the clean brilliance of color in that murky gray place, pierced by it so pain began to come back to him.

"It's after five, Yussel," Riebold called from the top of the steps. "Come on, we'll be on this all week anyhow."

Once he would have hurried at the lateness of the hour. Now he only looked regretfully at the dull shine of the pipe. Slowly he got to his feet. His knees ached.

"Okay," he breathed. "I'm coming."

The air felt cooler as he rode in the truck; it came in the open windows soothingly, drying the dirty sweat on Berman's face and bald head. It was suppertime, and the streets in the residential neighborhoods were empty and quiet. Occasionally, when they stopped at the corners, he could hear the voices from the houses, even the rattle of the dishes and cutlery.

"You sure you won't have supper at my house, Yussel?" Riebold asked for the third time. "Look, what's the harm? So you come over one night a week for supper. You know my Ethel would be crazy to have you. How 'bout it, Joe . . . no foolin', why not?"

"I'll tell you for the last time. Maybe later on, not now. First place, I don't want to start a routine like that. Once in a while, maybe. But right now, I'll do for myself. Same thing I told Ruthie. I got to try, work it out for myself. No one else can help." And then, as though remembering vaguely the shape of kindness, "Thanks, anyhow, Leo. Tell Ethel I appreciate, but not now."

He was even able to muster a small, bleak smile as he waved good-by to Riebold in front of his house. Then he watched the truck go slowly down the shadowed street, passing through the little patches of sunshine quickly as though preferring the cool shadows. It stopped at the corner and he could imagine Riebold peering carefully right and left on the empty streets until, satisfied at last that there were no cars within five blocks, he disappeared around the corner. Berman stood listening to the familiar loud motor until it was lost in the other distant sounds of the city.

And then he was alone with the whispering trees and his own long evening shadow, and the house stood mercilessly behind him.

First he kicked a few twigs from his sidewalk into the gutter. Then, halfway up the steps, he stopped to test the iron railing, shaking it vigorously as he squinted at the screws that held it. On the porch he picked up a few dead leaves and threw them

over the rail. He picked up the folded newspaper and studied
the little bit of headline visible. It read:

HWAY SLAUGHTER
OO OVERALL WEE

There was nothing else on the porch. He gave a little stricken
moan and looked at the door with dread.

CHAPTER THREE

The house was cool and musty like a place not lived in for thousands of years. Berman tried to disdain his feeling of guilt at coming in the front way in all his dirt. He ran a grimy hand spitefully over the brocaded armchair and then almost instinctively tried to brush at it.

He walked through the dining room, bent over a little, protectively, as though at a cramp in his stomach. He had the feeling that pain might come from the walls themselves.

In the bathroom he stripped his clothes off and washed his face, arms, chest, neck, and belly with water sloshed up from the sink. As he was drying his face, he caught sight of his eyes over the towel. They looked sly, and for a moment he had the feeling that it wasn't a mirror he gazed at but rather a window into a strange place from which some secretive stranger mimicked Berman and taunted him with the knowledge of a monstrous joke.

He put on a clean undershirt and a pair of stiffly immaculate khaki pants. Just as he sat on the edge of the tub, flexing his toes after the hot work shoes, he heard a creak in the back hall, seemed to catch a whiff of perfume. He stood up suddenly, his insides reverberating with an instant's joy. But then

he made a sour face at his insanity and shuddered at some un-
cleanness in himself.

The refrigerator held a patchy assortment of leftovers. He
hadn't thought about shopping for food since his daughter had
gone. There were three shriveled Brussels sprouts in a pyrex
dish, a piece of Swiss cheese getting hard at the edges from im-
proper wrapping, a few sardines congealing in their oil, a con-
tainer of sour cream and one of cottage cheese, an unopened
jar of herring, some pot roast, a piece of lemon meringue pie,
and several curled-up slices of beef tongue. He slammed the
refrigerator door in disgust and looked in the cupboard where
the groceries were kept.

In the end he settled on a dish of dry Rice Krispies, a can of
anchovies, and a glass of tea. He paid no attention to the
tastes in his mouth. Earnestly he tried to concentrate on the
minutiae of the kitchen; the stove handles, the sampler on the
wall that proclaimed "True Friendship Is a Gordian Knot
Which Angels' Hands Have Tied," even the pattern of the
linoleum occupied him, so it might have looked as though he
really were searching for something.

While he was washing his few dishes, the phone rang with
shocking volume in the stillness. It was his daughter, asking
how he was doing, whether he had worked, how he was
managing with his meals.

"Is it too awful, Daddy, really? I get sick just thinking of
you wandering around that house alone. Honestly, you would
be doing so much for me if you came here. Daddy, I still can't
get it through my head that she's gone. It's like a bad dream
that I keep expecting to wake up from. I go along doing my
housework, taking care of the kids, feeling everything is the
same. And then, bang, it hits me and I start to cry. I cry so
much, the kids don't understand. 'Why are you crying,
Mommy,' they say. Oh, Daddy, it must be ten times worse for
you, all alone there. . . ."

"No, no, I'm all right. It isn't as bad as you think. I worked today, a good job, real money. Then I came home, washed up good, relaxed, had a nice supper. . . ." It almost seemed real to him as he told it, an antiseptic little anecdote of a single man coming home to his comfortable house. "Now I'm gonna sit down, watch television, take it easy. I'm fine, Ruthie, don't worry."

"Did you shop for food? I'll bet you're still eating leftovers. Oh, Daddy . . . Well, one thing I insist on. You have to come here at least one night a week for supper."

"I'll talk to you tomorrow," Berman said, suddenly unable to go on with the conversation. He hung up the phone and stared at it for a minute, hanging on to the neatness he had manufactured for his daughter.

"All right," he said, looking around the room, leaning forward to see into the other rooms. "I can't live like a animal, walk like a crazy one through the rooms. . . ."

He went into the living room and eyed the books on the built-in shelves there. A strange assortment of titles met his eyes. He knew nothing of books except for the prayer books of his religion. Though he read English well enough to read the papers and the mail, he had always figured that reading a whole book in that language would be too involved. He reached for *Wuthering Heights* and turned to the first page of the story. After. a few seconds of trying to puzzle out the formal propriety of the sentences, he closed it and returned it to the shelves. He had heard of Tolstoy, so he opened the fat volume of *War and Peace,* but the first sentence made him think he was breaking into something already begun, so he put that away, too.

"Karamazov," he said with mild interest, recognizing the Russian sound of the name. This time he began to read aloud, hoping it would make more sense to him that way.

"Alexey Fyodorovitch Karamazov was the third son of

Fyodor Pavlovitch Karamazov, a landowner well known in our
district in his own day . . ."

For a little while he was interested in the story that took
place in the land of his birth. But then it all began to seem so
far back, another world, and the sound of the words began to
intrude on their meaning, so he stopped reading and put that
book back, too.

For a moment he mused inquisitively, wondering how long
ago he had stopped thinking in Yiddish and begun forming his
mental processes in English. "I am an *American,*" he said in a
mocking, sardonic voice, remembering how his wife used to
try lovingly to correct his pronunciation and how he would
pretend annoyance. Really he had been moved at her wistful
attempts to improve him, for he knew she loved him the way he
was and only wanted the rest of the world to be convinced of
his worth. "She was a simple woman," he said in a dull voice.

Suddenly his eyes fell on the gray window of the television
screen. He went over to it and switched it on, then sat down
tensely on the edge of the armchair watching the dot of light
slide sideways and explode silently into a rippled pattern which
finally adjusted to a recognizable image.

It was a children's program and he watched it motionlessly
for a while, not bothering to turn up the volume, so it seemed
he lived in deafness, seeing a world bright and monochromatic
and distant. He willed his interest to the scene and in a few
minutes, with the complete lack of distraction, found himself
immersed in the performance. First there was a juggler who
spun an amazing number of balls and sticks, then a trampoline
acrobat who bounced wondrously into the air. Berman sat with
his mouth open, a faint, rapt smile on his face. Finally a man
came out with a troop of small dogs and a monkey. He set the
dogs to running in a circle like horses in the circus and then,
amazingly, got the monkey to somersault from one moving back

to another. Mindless with the delight he had achieved and wishing as always to share it, he called out without turning.

"Mary—see this, Mary. . . ."

He strangled on his chuckle, felt it dissolve and chill his whole body with a grief that became astoundingly physical, and he sat shuddering and taut.

"Oh-h-h-h, oh. Oh, you shit God, you terrible filth. . . . Damn you, damn you," he said in a hoarse voice to the ceiling, his voice the only sound, the television flickering silently, meaningless now. "Such a deal you gave me, all my life. My eyes are open, you. You watched me pray every day of my life, saw me fast all the holy days, saw me be kind, loving, honest, you saw me take all the other rotten things and still go on loving you. And then you . . . you figured you could do anything to me . . . that I was a hopeless sucker . . . that I thanked you for the little bits you left me. And then you do this . . . and this in the worst way. No time for me to care for her before she went . . . to show her how many tears I had for her. . . . No, not even that, just *bang,* like clubbing an animal down . . . like an animal!" And then his voice got quiet, menacing, in the empty room. "I'm through with you, do you hear, *through!*"

But though this had sounded sonorous and composed of great lengths of tone when he said it, the words were echoless, disappearing suddenly as though into a muffling softness, and he looked around like a man trapped without atmosphere while the nonsensical light of the television played on the walls.

He felt a curiously porous freedom for a while. Divorced from something, he watched the screen numbly, seeing figures and familiar objects all as a sort of moving, meaningless montage. Finally he got up and shut the television off. He stood in the dimness feeling weary and inhuman.

"I'll take a sleeping pill," he said. "Else I wouldn't be able to work tomorrow." He walked through the darkening rooms, his hands out before him like a blind man's as though he doubted the familiar position of the chairs and tables. There was a burning red spot high on the window from the last of the sun reflected off the house next door. It only emphasized the darkness Berman walked through. In the kitchen, the little blue pilot light stared at his groping passage. Then down the long hall, past the bedrooms with their mute monuments of the lives lived in them, invisible now as he felt himself to be.

And then in the bathroom, the sudden silent burst of cloying light, the brightness of all the shiny-slick surfaces. His reflection blinked wildly from the pink mirror, the eyes with their pupils still enlarged by the recent darkness. For the while he felt he belonged in that hard, sparkling chamber as though he were made of porcelain himself.

He took the bottle of sleeping pills out of the medicine cabinet and poured the contents into his hand. There were two kinds, red and blue. The blue were the stronger, and he took one and put the remainder back in the bottle. He filled his hands with water from the sink and washed it down.

Almost immediately he felt the dizziness of the artificial drowse. He went into his own bedroom feeling almost cocky, fortified as he was by the sleeping pill. But when he lay down he realized that sleep was not as close as he had thought, so he held his eyes closed and tried to ignore the solitude of the wide bed.

May 7, 1954

Deep inside, under the sedation, was the pain. Somehow the drugs only made it worse, as though it were more horrible in its thin disguise. There was the pressure of the gas threatening to blow him up, and every so often he had to rock his head back and forth on the pillow in spite of Mary sitting there watching him.

"Do you want more water, Joe?" she asked, her face dear yet alien through the intimacy of his pain. The gas only came in crushing spasms, but the other, the place where they had cut while he lay trustfully sleeping, that went on and on as though it were a new part of him, as though something had been added to him instead of cut out. It isolated him from her, from his daughters murmuring to each other in the corner of the room. He had to imitate normal responses and expressions for them. It was as though they had become strangers to him, representations of things he knew he loved. But none of them was as close to him as the pain. God's hand inside me, he thought, not in those words, indeed not in words at all. All right, I have done enough bad things, I need reminding. I accept, I take this with love. . . . *Gott in Himmel . . . Baruch atah Adonoi . . .* God . . . GOD!

"Joe, Joe, what is it? Shall I call the doctor?" His wife's face hovered over him, lined, beautiful.

"It's all right . . . it's what they expect. In a few days it will let up. . . ." But he reached for her hand, which was something he rarely did.

And that tiny, unwonted gesture shook her and frightened her so she began to cry silently.

"It must be awful," she murmured sorrowfully.

"All right, all right." He dismissed it impatiently, a little strengthened by the touch of her hand. "Tell me . . . uh . . . how long is Debby going to stay? Debby, come here . . . you're visiting me. . . . Ruthie. . . ."

And for a while he sunned the surface of himself in his family's nearness, the sound of their feminine voices, nodding, managing pale smiles. He focused on them, shielded his eyes from the world of dark, writhing pain. It was like looking through a long pipe from some moldy cellar, looking up to see the disk of bright, sunny-blue sky. They talked about their homes, the daughters—their husbands and their babies; and their mother, Mary, commented, criticized, applauded. From both sides, careful not to touch the tubes that led into his body, they leaned carefully on the bed, so close that he could study their fine-pored skin, their lipsticks. Even their scents he could seize on for the moment, to the exclusion of that huge, inhuman odor of the hospital, a smell he imagined to be the breath of some great shiny machine filled with bright cutting blades.

Then finally they were gone. Over at the other end of the room an old man mewled his hazy pain from behind the white sidebars. Like a baby, Berman thought, both of us moaning in our cribs. Only the babies had just left oblivion, were waking up, and *they* were approaching it. Death—how close he felt to it, rended, burdened by pain, nourished tentatively by little rubber tubes, relieved by others. He was so close that he was beyond terror, like being in so close under a beast's jaws that it cannot reach you but only can click its teeth menacingly in your ear, warning you that only inches save you.

The hospital grew quiet with a hospital's peculiar somnolence of the late hours. Really it wasn't quiet at all. Activity went on all night, yet you were aware of the spirit of sleep being urged, coaxed on all the restless patients. Moans rippled in uneven rhythm through the halls; there were whispered conversations between nurses, clinking glasses, the surreptitious hiss of rubber-tired wheels, the occasional bump of the elevator doors, and then the uninitiated loudness of a new patient's voice, crying or screaming or just questioning.

Berman lay in the dimness of the night-lit room, his neck arched against the pain, his mouth wide and shocked, his eyes puzzled, trying to understand the sense of his agony, feeling the squeezing hand of God inside, punishing, punishing. . . .

"Baruch atah Adonoi elohanu melech . . ."

The student nurse came in at the sound of him.

"Little uncomfortable, Mr. Berman? Well, Nursie has a nice little pill for you. . . ."

And Berman continued the prayer silently, not in the least comforted by her prattle. He let himself be exposed like a baby and moved around by the girl who didn't know enough to be ashamed before a man's nakedness. And then he reeled toward the black, unnatural sleep of the pill, receded from the dim, whispering, comfortless hospital and the sounds of the old man mewling, all the other sufferers.

He prayed as long as he was conscious and then did nothing for many hours.

His sleep was like a seamless cylinder. The opiate sealed him in and dreams were distant things like faint sounds outside it. Something threatened, the sleep itself. It was coffin-like, black and heedless as space. From within its dark confines he railed against it, scratched desperately at it as though with his finger-nails on its massive lid. He strained for human consciousness, to know, to know. . . .

And finally he raised the cover of massive slumber. Just a little at first, his eyelids leaden, his mouth thick and dry. The sleep tugged at him but he fought, strained out of it. Something abominable was in the room with him, someone or something.

Slyly he ranged his eyes over the moonlit confusion of the bedroom without moving his body. The hulking darkness of the high dresser, the lower bureau . . . But that, that shadow— what was that? Sweat began at the roots of his hair, his flesh tingled with a thrill of fear. Slowly, ever so slowly, he moved his hand toward the lamp. He felt the edge of the night table, the bumpy lace of the little cloth, and then he recoiled in horror at the feel of soft, fine *hair*.

"Yaaaa-aaaa . . ." He screamed. The lamp crashed to the floor and he jumped to his feet and ran over the little pieces of glass to the hallway. In the kitchen he switched the light on and ran to the counter where the drawers were. He jerked the drawer open too far in his haste and it fell to the floor. From the spilled things he seized a long, straight-bladed knife, and, bent over like a killer, walked back to the bedroom.

He reached into the room from the hallway, found the switch, and, with the knife held murderously before him, turned it on. His heart stopped in anticipation of horror.

But the room was empty of life and death. The familiar furniture he had lived with for more than thirty years stood patiently, forgiving everything. He swept his eyes slowly past the picture of himself at twenty-five—dark, lean, homely in a vigorous, humorous way; past her picture at about the same age—full-faced, flawless, like some large-headed flower. And then he looked at the night table from which he had knocked the lamp.

The only thing there was the small, crumpled softness of a hair net. He walked over to it and picked it up, felt its frailty in his huge, coarse hand and studied it through the distortion of his tears. He noticed the knife in his other hand and threw it from him with a cry of guilt.

"Did I think it was her returned to me? And if I did, what was my fear . . . why the knife? Would I kill her again?" And then he sat on the edge of the bed with the hair net up to his mouth and cried bitterly, dazed and weary with his grief beyond trying for comprehension.

At last he was dried of tears again and trembling with a slow, steady palsy as though with great age. Tenderly he put the hair net back on the table. With a deep breath he renewed himself for the strengthening hatred. Firmly he raised his head and bent his mouth in a vicious sneer.

"Go ahead, go on, soon I'll be able to take worse. . . . With my last breath I will curse you. Ha, you overdid yourself. I'm getting too small a target for you. You did everything—almost, anyhow. Soon maybe you will kill my children and then what will you do? You'll be like a child kicking a dead bird. There'll be no satisfaction. . . . What do you do then, you, supposed to be such a big God."

Then, feeling physically strong in spite of the persistent trembling, he went back into the kitchen to get the dustpan and brush. He swept up the broken glass and dumped it and the wreckage of the lamp into the trash bag. He noticed that he must have cut his feet on the glass when he first bolted from the bed. Great flat, bloody prints led from the room to the kitchen and back. He got a rag and wiped the floor clean, crawling on his knees like a penitent, following the dark-crimson smears. He picked up the contents of the kitchen drawer and put everything away.

In the bathroom he washed his feet and wrapped gauze around them. Then he urinated, noticing idly that he felt no pain this time.

The trembling persisted, so he began walking through the house from back to front and back again. On the second tour he stopped outside his daughters' room and after a moment went in to sit on one of the twin beds there.

He looked around at the oversweet, feminine decor. His wife and daughters had striven for some kind of colonial delicacy. The twin beds had the tall, elaborately turned posts and the nubby, coarse linen bedspreads that the magazines called early American. On the wall beside one bed were little oval-framed snapshots of the girls when they were two and three, and, on the side he was on, similarly framed silhouettes in black paper of no one in particular. There were little flowered jars on the dressers, a mirrored tray, and a vanity Berman had got for his older daughter, Ruth, on her fifteenth birthday. Slowly he eased himself back onto the hard, taut roll of the pillow, careful not to muss the neat, wrinkleless surface of the spread.

Gradually his trembling left him. He began to relax there in the room that had known much girlish laughter, that chamber from which had issued the smells of powder and toilet water and all the other fragile yet strong essences of girlhood. He used to come home from work, still in his grime and shabbiness from the job, to stand almost breathlessly outside their doorway, careful not to be seen, exulting like a miser listening to the clinking of his treasure. His son had never quite achieved that same preciousness for him, because his son had been, after all, like himself, male, coarse-grained . . . like himself.

He gave a great sigh as he felt his eyes roll upward and his body grow weighted again with fatigue and the remains of the opiate he had taken hours before.

"Oy vay, oh-h-h-h-h." He yawned shudderingly, and started down the incline.

Berman walked up the shell-lined path to the restaurant, holding his wife's arm so she wouldn't trip in the darkness. Otherwise he wasn't prone to such amenities, any more than he was to terms of endearment or cuteness in demonstrations of affection for his daughters. "You always are worried about your dignity," his wife would say teasingly sometimes. "Some men call their wives 'honey' or at least 'dear.' But not you, not my big, tough plumber." And he would respond, with his heavy-handed slapstick humor, "Oh, honey sweetheart darling, I luff you, I luff you, I'm dying with lufff-fff. . . ." So his daughters and wife would squeal with laughter and Mary would end up wiping her eyes as she shook her head at his childishness. But tacitly they would have to agree, by their looks of love, that he was right, that they wouldn't want him any other way.

The waves pounded on the beach far down the street and

there was a smell of salt and rank mud and seaweed. He felt
he shouldn't have agreed to his daughters' suggestion that they
all go out to dinner. His mother had taken sick two days before
and was now lying in an oxygen tent in the hospital, her
clouded eyes bewildered in the clinical dimensions of the hospital room. She spoke very poor English and had begged her
son to "tell the nurses about me, they should know I do not
speak their language, they should know what to do. . . ." At
first he had been at a loss, had been reluctant even to leave the
room. But then Mary had discovered that one of the student
nurses was Jewish, and they sent the girl in to converse with
the old lady, who responded with smiles from inside the transparent tent which made her look like some ancient specimen
preserved from another time.

"I know she's old. It's not the way she is now that hurts
me. She will die, probably soon, and I will know that it will be
the best thing for her, so old and foggy and full of pain she is.
No, it is not for that old woman that I cry inside. It is for how
I remember her, how she cared for me when I was a boy. . . ."
And he had shrugged and accepted the stiff white shirt Mary
proffered.

But his heart wasn't in it and he gave a harassed sigh as he
held the door of the restaurant open for his wife.

"Where's the kids?" he asked as he went ahead to open the
inner door.

"They said they would meet us, they would get here early
for a table."

Berman ran his eyes over his wife's figure, bright and trim
in a blue dress. Nothing showed on his face, but he followed
her erect body with a deadpan pride. He knew the little col-
lapses of her body, the age-ugly folds and wrinkles, and he
loved and revered her all the more for the neat, attractive ex-
terior she was still capable of. She was just the more irrevoca-

bly his in her hidden imperfections, for only he knew them. He was her proud ally in the public appearance.

When he first stepped into the main dining room, he was a little blinded by the brightness, saw nothing in any detail he could connect to. So he was really startled by the sudden roar of the crowd, tensed himself as though he might have walked into a trap set by enemies. It was at least a half-minute before he was able to make out what their cry was and by then they were surrounding Mary and him, pummeling, hugging, kissing.

"Happy anniversary, Bermans . . . *mazel tov* . . . should have fifty more . . . luck . . . luck. . . ."

Then he was kissing his daughters, shiny-eyed in their delight at bringing off the surprise, choked with sentiment, pride. He and Mary were led to a table at one end of the big room and an orchestra began playing a tune that made his wife cry out with pleasure and nostalgia. He had to get out on the dance floor and dance with her and then with a half-dozen other partners, his daughters included.

He swam in a sea of voices and laughter, turned this way and that, with a constant smile wearying his mouth to oblige his well-wishers. He had a drink with this old friend and that one, with a relative he hadn't seen in fifteen years, and with one he saw on the street every other day and to whom he rarely had anything to say. He had one drink with his wife and one each with each of his daughters' boy friends. A dazzle came before his eyes and he told himself it was one of the great evenings of his life. Only it was a little too much; he would have liked to celebrate with a few less people. But still . . . how nice it was . . . how wonderful of all of them. . . . He kissed his wife to oblige them, laughed at their innocently lewd jokes, agreed that *it* was better than ever now after a quarter of a century, and drank some more.

After a while he sat at the table over a drink, nodding his

head at the conversation of a few very old friends. His partner, Riebold, sat with his arm around Berman's shoulder, recalling some wicked adventure of their younger days.

"Remember your face when that hotel door swung open? . . ."

And Berman nodded in the noisy, smoky room, with the band playing fiercely some wild old *hora* and the glasses clinking and the feet stomping out on the dance floor and the smell of women's powder and men's sweat.

Yet under it all, distant and faint now as the sound of the sea outside, a tiny rhythmic crashing of sadness beat like a little pulse inside him. He was happy but there was all of that, too, the sadnesses, the losses, things he hardly thought of in the midst of his routine days; but here, in the midst of celebration, they made themselves known as though by contrast alone, like a cool current running against your body while you bathe in some warm stream.

And finally it was over. They went out into the cool evening. The stars shone high over the water and the darkened shapes of the distant amusements—the roller coaster, the great whirling machines. Berman heard the echo of all the voices ringing in his ears. Besides, he was a little drunk, and his daughters and Mary were laughing at him, their voices small in the depths of sea-damp air.

All the way back to town he sang Russian songs, wild, shouting songs, sad, plaintive ones. They laughed and applauded, his wife and daughters and the boy friends, so he sang all the louder while the car rocked through the starry night.

Happy, yes, I'm happy, he exulted, despite the thin, cool current of sadness. And he sang and sang . . . until they were home and his daughters were gone to spend the night with the family of one of the boy friends and Mary shushed him into the dark house.

"Don't shush me," he said. "This is my house, my own house. I'm king here."

She giggled in the bedroom as they undressed, two middle-aged people still shy of their bodies before each other.

Berman felt that cool current and suddenly he felt desperate for something in the night, something elusive that had trailed him all evening, had winked brightly at various moments like mysterious gems in a river bed: in the Russian songs, the ocean sounds, the flash of his wife's proud blue dress.

Hungrily he reached for the familiar warmth beside him, ran his hands over the large, sagging breasts, the deep, warm belly and body hair.

"Oh, Joe," she said in loving surprise. "Do you really want to . . . can you?" She turned and pressed close and soft to him.

Physically the act was slow and arduous. Berman worked at it, not helped by all the liquor he had consumed. But if the love-making hadn't the grace and ease and beauty of the days of their youth, it had something more, something which could survive the awkwardness of the heavy-breathing, aging man coupling with the thickening wife. For there was a solemnity, an awesome sense of commemoration in their silent act of love, and when Berman finally rolled over and lay listening to their mingled breathing as it receded from passion, his body and mind were touched with youth and he locked hands with his wife in mutual gratitude.

In a little while her steady exhalations told him she had fallen asleep. Berman lay studying the slatted shadows of the Venetian blinds cast over their bodies by the moonlight. He was happy, very happy, but there was that sadness ahead and behind. The losses, they were like very faint voices in the still of the night—the son, the father, soon the mother. . . .

Tears lay in cool streaks on his cheeks when he finally drifted off to sleep with his wife's warm hand in his.

CHAPTER FIVE

He woke early with a cold taste in his mouth. Quickly he dressed in his work clothes and rushed out of the house as though hoping to move so rapidly that he might escape the feel of the empty rooms.

The air was fresh and cool with morning. Bird song made a subdued din in the trees over his head and the sidewalks were laved with the long slant of the early sun. He stood uncertainly before the house, feeling large and rough and alien in the sweet air. It was so early that he could hear no human sounds except one distant truck motor many blocks away. Part of him took a thin delight in the beauty of the day but that very pleasure also imbued him with an even more terrible loneliness. At least in the house he was consumed by struggle, occupied by the goading objects of his loss. But out here he was a solitary creature in a world of joined human beings. He pictured how he might look to some woman gazing curiously out of her window, still heavy with sleep—a big, slouched figure, his coarse-featured face shadowed by the down-turned brim of the shabby, sweat-stained fedora he always wore to work, disdaining bareheadedness or the more popular sporty caps many of the men affected; menacing, restless, all wrong on that fresh, quiet street of sleeping families and quiet little lawns. Spite-fully he felt a desire to let out a great furious roar, to make them know Berman and his awesome, burning rage.

He didn't know the time but guessed it was at least an hour and a half before Riebold would come. Slowly he began walk-ing. A milk truck passed him, stopped somewhere behind him. There came a rattle of bottles, the crash of a heavy milk crate. A dog barked in one of the yards and farther off a screen door slammed. There was a deep self-disgust in him at the thought of his aimless meandering through the dawn. "Berman the bum," he said with bitter humor.

Finally he came to a little luncheonette. The owner was just bringing in the newspapers left there during the night. There was dew on the plate-glass window. The man looked puffy with sleep.

"Good morning," he said to Berman.

"Got some coffee yet?" Berman asked.

"Got it on the fire. Give it five minutes. Come on in, read the paper while you're waiting."

Berman followed him in. The coffee odor tingled in his nose. It made him smile slightly. The proprietor's voice seemed to have great charm to him. He tried to hear it again.

"What time is it?" he asked the man.

"There's a clock up there . . . 'bout five minutes fast. Must be pretty close to quarter of seven. . . . Go ahead, sit down." He tossed a paper in front of Berman. "Have a look-see what's goin' on in the world."

"Thanks, thanks," Berman said, full of gratitude for the warm smell and the peculiarly charming sound of the human voice. "Think I'll take you up. . . ."

He sat there drinking the hot coffee and reading the front-page stories of disaster. His body relaxed and he thought about nothing except his effort to read the smudgy print. For a little while a transparent, superficial peace lay over him like the early sunshine that fell on his shoulders through the plate-glass window.

Someone else came into the store. There was a murmur between the newcomer and the proprietor.

"Who's he?" said a rude, gravelly voice.

Berman looked in the mirror to see a policeman staring suspiciously at him. He looked at his own reflection in the mirror, saw the rough, brooding, unshaved face under the grimy hat, the menacing lines of suffering on his cheeks. His rage split through the brief layer of calm. He spun around on the stool and stood up facing the policeman.

"Ask me, don't ask him. I'm Berman, Berman, that's who I am!" Then he slapped a quarter down on the counter and stalked out, shaken with anger.

Behind him he heard the proprietor tell the police officer, "He's all right, lives in the neighborhood. . . ." And the policeman, mollified, grumbling, "Well, what the hell got into him, flying up like that. . . ."

He waited on his front steps for Riebold, his eyes glazed against the passers-by, his ears deafened to the voices of children testing the day. In his own private darkness brought out of the night, he sat waiting in the growing light of the sun.

That day they worked their way up through the various odorous apartments of the old building, breaking walls, ripping out rusting pipe in some places, putting in long, sinuous sections of gleaming copper tubing, plastering, lifting, twisting mightily at the heavy Stillson wrenches. Much of the time they had an audience. In one flat, a half-blind old man offered a running stream of advice.

"Yuh got to put plenny ob dat stickum on dem joints. Keeps 'em from leakin'. . . . Turn 'em good an' tight now, you strong young fellas . . . got to turn 'em tight. . . ."

And in the apartment above, the buxom young mother of the house stood watching Berman with sleepy interest, her round, dark arms crossed under her huge, pillow-like breasts. Her children pushed in and out of the room and Berman was constantly reaching around and over their dark, woolly heads for his tools. "Okay, sweetie," he would say, clasping a pipe-stem arm and pulling gently. "Now you watch your step, little boy. . . ."

The whole building was filled with the poor smell of cabbage and mold, yet it was a reek oddly vital. Berman breathed it with a sort of wistful annoyance, and after a while found a taunt in it that made him scowl and mutter peevishly to Riebold, *"Fashtunkina Shwartsa* cooking . . . piuu!" But Riebold only shrugged good-naturedly, not recognizing the apparent scorn in his partner's voice for the yearning it really was.

The workingmen of the house were home and drinking beer in their undershirts before Riebold and Berman decided to quit for the day. As Berman collected his tools, he saw one young Negro bouncing a child on each knee. The plump young woman who had watched them work, apparently his wife, walked by him and the young man reached out past the children to seize one vast buttock in a playful squeeze. The sound of her laughter trailed out behind them as they drove off in the truck, and it seemed to Berman that it rang faintly in the van behind him as though someone had tapped sharply on one of the lengths of pipe.

His son-in-law was waiting for him on the front steps. For a moment after he waved good-by to Riebold, Berman felt a wonderful sensation of relief at the thought of not having to go into the house alone. Then he frowned.

"What's wrong?" he asked the young man.

His son-in-law smiled.

"Nothing's wrong. Don't you remember you're supposed to come to us for supper tonight? Come on. Ruthie's waiting for us."

"Yes, yes, all right. I'll wash up and change my clothes.

Come in with me, I'll only be a few minutes." And they both
went into the house, which only echoed their brief time there
like a public place.

His daughter's house was large and modern. Berman used
to complain that it was "cold," with its spare, unembellished
furniture and big areas of white wall. They had always laughed
at his suggestion that they put in some "knickknack shelfs and
soft armchairs to warm up a little. . . ." And he had good-
naturedly joined their laughter, mocking himself for forgetting
they lived in a different world and saw things differently.

They ate with the mild pandemonium of three young children storming in and out of the dining room. Berman ate more
avidly than he had expected, realizing suddenly how little he
had eaten since his daughter left his house. And then, with the
comfort of the food in his stomach, he held his grandson on
his knee and gave himself over to the warmth and balm of the
medley of voices, soothed, mercifully dulled to thought. He
helped put his grandchildren to bed, paying particular attention to the long-faced little boy, who had large, melancholy
eyes which most unexpectedly turned twinkling and humorous
when he smiled.

But when he stood over the children, all rosy in their beds,
while his daughter fussed, proud before him, with windows and
strewn clothes, he felt a peculiar pang at his back, almost a
stiffening as though from a spectral draft; so he stalked suddenly from the room as though guilty at coveting something
that was not all his.

Later his son-in-law drove him home through the summer
moonlight. He stood before his house for a minute or two,
listening to the dreamlike hiss of hoses and lawn sprinklers,
and the voices of all the people communing in the warm evening on porches or strolling along the sidewalk past him, arms
or hands linked or just joined by glances and murmurs. A
Good Humor truck came, slowly jingling its bells, white and

solemn like a bearer of something strange—some message, some memory. Berman stood there on the slumberous street, immobilized by the muted voices and the sweet smell of cut grass and flowers, all of it concentrated into a thin, hard shaft of life that pierced him like a foolish, impossible dream, a thing as beyond him as the fairy tales of his childhood.

In the house he shut all the windows against the scent of the earth and the blossoms. Then he set some water to boiling. He wasn't hungry after all he had eaten at his daughter's house. Rather he had some impulse to wash his mouth of all the good, burdening tastes of the food. The kitchen relieved him, put him in a mournful sort of ease with its shining, clinical coldness.

While he sipped at the cup of hot water he studied a calendar. The pictures at the tops of the pages distracted him for a while. They were lovely color photographs of various parts of the United States in one or another of the seasons. There was a spray-filled ocean beach, a blue-hazed mountain, and a broad river glinting in a summer sun, which he studied the longest as though trying to place where he might have seen it before.

Finally he concentrated on the dates.

"I'll count the days to six months," he muttered. "I told Ruthie six months. . . ." He got up and went to the cupboard drawer where the cards and pads and stubs of pencils had always been kept. There was a cheap plastic fan there. It had the words "Souvenir Old Orchard Beach" on it. She used to suffer terribly from extremes of heat or cold. He remembered her sitting on the back porch, sighing in the dark as she waved the fan back and forth.

Almost savagely, he crossed off the days since his daughter's departure. His last slashing mark ripped the paper, destroyed the day. Impatiently he threw the calendar over to the counter and took his empty glass to the sink.

The worn linens on the bed were cool. He lay back on the pillow with his hands behind his head. The air in the room was still and odorless with the windows closed. There were no ghosts in the room, there was nothing but the large, aging body of a man who stared flatly at the ceiling.

"You went too far this time. Even a dog learns after you keep pulling his bone away time after time. Even a dummy like Berman can learn the score. I will curse you every night, do you hear! Instead of prayers I will curse you." His mouth bent in a horrible smile. "Dog, *hoont,* devil—may you rot and make a stink for the whole universe to smell forever. . . ."

And his voice continued, shallow and echoless in the closed-in room, soft, maniacal, filled with all the hatred he could muster, coming out in obscenities that had no meaning or sense, so they became, after a while, a sort of background noise to him, a grim, ugly lullaby which began to make him drowsy.

April 17, 1945

It seemed he had a film over his eyes all the time lately. The steady screeching of all the machines in the factory was just a hum in its constancy. He supposed it had to do with tiredness, that dullness of perception, and even of touch. Not that he really *felt* tired, experienced any loss of strength or uncommon desire for sleep. Yet, he reasoned as he stood at one end of the huge, concrete-floored room, watching as befitted an inspector, three and a half to four hours of sleep in twenty-four over a period of two years . . . it had to accumulate, add up to some loss of power. The busyness of his schedule *was* oppressive when he thought about it. He watched the many lathes turning, saw the gleaming cylinders and cones of the artillery shells shaping, reaching their grim maturity; and as though in defense against the thought of their uses, of the war and his son involved in it somewhere, he ran idly through the monotonous program of his days. The plumbing work was negligible, materials were so hard to come by. He and Riebold chased around for their scattered jobs and were usually done by two o'clock in the afternoon. At three in the afternoon, home and washed clean, Berman went to sleep. At six-thirty or seven, Mary woke him for dinner. They sat around the table, he and his wife and two daughters, exchanging remarks on school, boys, the war, the mail, and their various friends and acquaintances. They wondered anxiously where his son was in relation to the headlines, whether his older daughter should get a new dress for a high-school dance or the younger one should go out with a boy five years her senior. They argued, laughed, commiserated. Sometimes Berman had to raise his voice, occasionally even his hand. One or another of the girls might retire from the table in tears, his wife might sulk for as long as an hour. They all helped with the dishes and later Berman and his wife played Michigan rummy as they listened to the radio, only pausing in their game when the news or special announcements came on. At ten o'clock they had coffee and cake. Berman told a story about something that had happened the day before. His older daughter teased him for his thinning hair. Finally he put on his shirt and windbreaker, his old hat. His wife kissed him good-by playfully, teasing because they all knew he disliked those little sentimentalities. Each of his daughters kissed him and he pretended annoyance as he shoved them away. They called out their good-bys, a medley of girlish voices, his wife's indistinguishable from theirs, and Berman waved them off impatiently. Only outside did he permit himself a little smile. Then, walking to the bus, feeling a little foolish but dedicated enough not to let that stop him, he murmured a prayer for his son's safety. By eleven he was at the factory, calling out his tough, joking answers to the wisecracks of the men on his shift over the screaming machines. The light, harsh and false, carved every experience out of men's faces. He stopped here and there with his micrometer, checking, advising, arguing. It was like a great underground cavern; the night outside the huge,

screened windows could have been solid rock, so palpable and
confining was it. Somewhere, above the place they labored in,
was the real world, rocked by terrible explosions, full of the
killing savagery. His son was there. He made ammunition for
his son's weapons. Pure and simple; awful, too.

Now, at about four in the morning, as he sipped coffee from
a paper cup, he felt the ending of one day's cycle approaching.
He would settle for that, for the constant din of machinery, the
ever-present weariness. Nothing worse, please God. He didn't
even dare dream of better things for fear of disturbing his precarious luck.

One of the workers, a rangy Negro in his fifties, flashed his
scattered teeth in a grin.

"Yo, Berman, how dey hangin'?"

"Go on, you," Berman shouted, his eyes amused.

An Italian with a wolf's face shrilled, "Oy oy, Berman, oy
oy, d' inspector Berman."

"Go on, Luksh, choke on spaghetti," Berman yelled back.
"You're sabotaging the war effort." Then more comfortably
he settled back on the swivel chair to survey his domain.

Far down the room two figures appeared. Berman strained
to make them out, wondered if it could be the superintendent.
One of them wore a blue uniform—one of the guards; but who
was that with him. That burly bear's figure—Riebold. What
was he doing here? His brow furrowed, Berman wallowed in
puzzlement, kept himself submerged in a counterfeit surprise
even after he had sensed the first touch of alarm.

"What the hell are you doing here?" he shouted. "You want
a job or something!" He forced a big grin which felt ridiculous
and false. The guard stood by with his head averted, embarrassed at knowing something not yet revealed to Berman.
"All right, Riebold, what's up—a job, a flooded cellar? I can't
take off now, you know that!" The grin was hurting his mouth
now. He didn't dare turn it off. Something terrible would ap-

pear if he did. He knew it. "You want some coffee, come on, sit down." He pushed his partner into a chair.

"Yussel," Riebold said in a cracked voice. His face was white.

"It's okay, Finnel," Berman said to the guard. "You don't have to stay, I know him. He's a Nazi spy but I can handle him."

"Yussel, you have to listen to me," Riebold said, leaning forward in the chair. "Please . . ." There were tears in his eyes.

"Sure, sure, big deal. Let me pour you some coffee." He poured a cupful from the big Thermos. The corners of his smile were throbbing now. "Comin' down here to watch me work, hah! Get some free coffee. . . . Okay, okay, it can wait. . . . Sit down and visit awhile, you old lazy bum, comin' down to watch hard-workin' men work while you sit on your ass. Hah, I know you, Riebold. . . ." He punched Riebold's arm and winked at the guard, who retreated a few steps. Finally he gave a wild little chuckle. "What's the matter, your wife bores you, gotta come down here and annoy me."

"Yussel, Yussel, it's no use clowning. I got to tell you, you got to sit down and listen," Riebold said, his cheeks streaming. "Please, Yussel, please."

And suddenly Berman sank down onto the chair and let out every bit of air in his body. There seemed to be no life in his body at all. Yet there was a horrid feeling of relief, too, as though the tightrope he had trodden so tensely and so long had snapped and crashed him to the ground. He had the monstrous pain but the tension was gone.

"Don't tell me," he said in a low, dry voice which, oddly enough, was perfectly audible to Riebold and the guard. "I know it all. My Marvin is dead, dead. That's what you came to tell me. My son is dead and now I know. You came to tell me and now I know, so there's nothing else you can do, no one can do. . . ." For a minute, like a reflex, the smile came back to his mouth, grotesque and putrid like something dug up from the ground. "Aha," he said. "Aha, aha, aha, aha hahahaaaaa . . ." And he began to wail like an animal stricken in the groin.

Some of the faces at the machines turned that way. A few machines shut off, and the noise was slightly lessened. They watched with curious pity as the guard and Riebold led Berman down the long corridor past all the machines. The wailing made them wince. It sickened them a little.

"God help me, help me," Berman whimpered in the spring evening as they helped him into the truck. The April breeze touched him with its terrible awakening smell. "God in heaven help me," he cried, making Riebold cry aloud too as he drove.

"Now, Yussel, Yussel, please, that won't help, please. . . ."

Berman rocked back and forth on the seat, his arms around himself, hugging, his face in a comical grimace under his tears. He thought of his son's body as it had been when he was a child—thin, olive-skinned, flawless. . . . Torn now, destroyed . . . To know why . . . why . . . Such pain, such pain. He had never dreamed there could be pain like that. It crushed him, wrenched his bones, trod on his brain. And he knew what made the pain so much worse, so unimaginably worse. No one else knew, only he, only he. He had sinned, he had been guilty. He had loved his son less than his daughters, had given him less of himself. Now he would pay, how he would pay. For eternity he would suffer remorse along with his grief. Oh my God, the endlessness of my loss, forever.

And the truck rocked through the dark early morning, the tires whining a little on the dew-dampened pavements, the smell of the earth yielding up life, the sound of the branches with their painful buds moving in the wind, and Berman's steady, ceaseless cry of puzzlement and grief carried through the sleeping city like the voice of the earth itself.

He used to wonder at callousness and brutality in people, never had been able to understand it or believe in it. But tonight, coming into the horrible emptiness of the house with the smell of sewage still in his nostrils, he felt somehow changed. There was a bleak satisfaction in inflicting the solitude on himself. It was a Friday night. He sat down in the living room in his soiled clothing. Desecration appealed to him suddenly. Cruelly he ran his dirty hands over the little doilies on the arms of the chair.

"Friday night," he said aloud. *"Shabbas ba nacht,* a holy night, holy hah!"

He looked around him threateningly, studied every memento with an eye to destruction. "Dead is gone, all right. . . . Nothing . . . Hah, God? So why not . . . shit on it all. . . ."

There was a deep, nauseating sickness in him, an oppressiveness, a ghostly pain in his stomach—no, his heart, his lungs, everywhere.

He began crying, harsh, brainless crying which did nothing to relieve him, only made him despise himself. Don't worry, he

said silently, don't rub your hands like you got something on
me. Just my nerves are shot, my body is tired.

"Huh . . . huh . . . huh . . . huh . . . huh . . ." came the
wrenching sobs, despicable, shameful stutters of his racked
body.

Suddenly the phone rang. He raced for it, almost stumbling
over a chair on the way. The tears coursed a clean path on his
cheeks in the midst of the gray dirt. The knees of his pants were
slippery with grease.

"Who is it?" he demanded.

"It's me, Daddy. Were you sleeping or something? It sounds
like you're sleepy or out of breath or something. Are you all
right?"

"I'm fine."

"What are you doing; did you just get home or what?"

"No, no, I'm sitting and relaxing. I'm all washed up and
clean, had a nice supper. Now I'm gonna sit and watch television . . . fine, comfortable. . . ." He stared at the stump of his
amputated finger, noticing how the dirt didn't cling to the shiny-
smooth scar tissue. Idly he tried to draw some conclusion from
that but was distracted by the effort to keep his shuddering sobs
from his daughter's notice. He was no longer crying but the
spasms continued, more as though he were permanently
chilled.

"Daddy, I have an idea. I really wish you would agree with
it. I want you to come here for dinner on Tuesday nights and
Friday nights. Bob will come for you and bring you home. It
will break up the week for you and I want to see you, I need
you. I'm so lonely, Daddy, you have no idea. . . ."

"Not Friday nights," Berman rasped. Oh, no, that night was
dedicated to his war, to his hatred. He realized how harsh he
sounded. "Tuesdays maybe, for now just Tuesdays. Later on
we'll see . . . okay . . . we'll see." He watched his neighbor, all
dressed in gardening hat and shorts, fussing with his ridiculous

little yard. He was edging the ground around the small fruit tree. You could see it was the most important thing in the world to him.

"Daddy?" his daughter said in his ear as though afraid he had hung up.

"Yes . . ."

"Daddy, I have another idea. Now hear me out and don't jump down my throat before you think about it. You don't have to do it immediately, but think about it."

"All right, say, say it."

"It's just this, and I think it might be a very good thing." She hesitated as though preparing to plunge into something that might be painful for both of them. "I think you should consider taking in a boarder."

Berman was silent. His mouth was twisted in a scornful smile at the sight of his neighbor puttering around the tiny tree.

"At least you wouldn't rattle around in an empty house, go crazy with loneliness. Just to have another face, a voice . . . You could use the money, too. It certainly wouldn't hurt."

"It's crazy," he said flatly. "Don't be ridiculous."

"Daddy, you said you would at least think about it."

"You said it. *I* said nothing."

"Please, Daddy, one thing I ask? It's for my peace of mind, too. I'd feel better to know you weren't alone. All I ask is that you think about it. That's not too much to ask, is it?"

"All right, Ruthie, all right. I'll think about it. I will. Give the kids a kiss for me, say hello to Bobby." He hung up in the middle of her farewell.

His face was malevolent as he went in all his filth to the bedroom and lay down on the immaculate, soft blanket. His shoes had bits of ash clinging to the soles. He saw the dirt soil the blanket. He felt masked with grease, except for the long lines of naked skin where his tears had run, like rents in the covering of dirt on his face.

Foul, a big hulking shape of filth in the clean, pretty room. Blackness filled his head, clouded out behind his eyes like ink spreading through water. He thought he was experiencing Hell. His body was a stench of evil in his nose. He thought of decay and rot and suffered indescribable pains, pains that traveled to every part of his body yet were not quite real enough to occupy him.

"Go on, go on," he called to the ceiling. "Do everything. Here I am, kill me, kill me." And he lay hopefully spread-eagled, eyes upward, offering himself to some kind of crucifixion.

Outside there was the peaceful, chewing groan of his neighbor's lawnmower, interrupted from time to time by the little pling of a stone hitting the whirling blades.

July 22, 1934

He and Riebold usually quit working a little before four in the summer. They shared a big cottage with their families down at the beach and it was an eight-mile ride from the city.

Riebold sat naked from the waist up, his thick-muscled torso carpeted with black hair. He sang over the rattle of the truck motor and beat time to his discordant solo on the big wooden steering wheel. Berman smiled a little. He had also taken off his shirt in the terrific heat but he wore an undershirt over his hairless, remarkably white body. He tried to rest his arm on the door but the metal was burning hot. Even the wind of their passage was a warm breath of heated tar and pavement. The trolley tracks were fiery ribbons leading them to the shimmering distance. The people they passed moved slowly, resigned to the harsh dream of summer. Only the children had the secret of vigor. They clustered around sprinklers and hoses, swarmed like flies around the backs of ice wagons.

And then, suddenly, with no apparent change of scene, the

air was somewhat cooler and the faint but unmistakable odor of salt and tideland reached them.

"Gonna take me a nice swim as soon as we get there," Riebold said. "Nice long easy swim . . ."

"It's not high tide till after supper," Berman said.

"Who cares? I'll walk out a little. Oh boy, just to wet my feet . . . I'm melting." He turned to his partner. Berman looked oddly cool in his undershirt, with his white skin. "Christ, you don't hardly sweat at all."

"A lot of the heat is in your head, too, you know. You walk around moaning, wiping your head, drinking gallons of water. No wonder you sweat like that."

"Ah, Yussel, you're made of ice."

"Not where it counts I'm not. Mary will tell you."

"Go on, Yussel, you're all talk." Riebold chuckled, jabbing his partner's arm.

"Okay, you make your wife think that so she don't get jealous of my Mary." Berman returned the punch a little harder and Riebold punched back. For a few seconds they grappled in the front seat. Then the truck swerved. Riebold seized the wheel hurriedly as a policeman wagged a threatening finger. Berman started to laugh and Riebold joined him. They shook and screeched their merriment until they rounded the curve that brought them in sight of the sea, and then relinquished their laughter for quiet, contented smiles, which they wore the rest of the way to the summer town.

They greeted their wives in the rich-smelling air of the kitchen. Riebold's wife was thin and sandy-haired and there was a devilish humor in her hazel eyes. She tickled the hairy chest of her husband as she kissed him, and he squealed as he lumbered out to the bathhouse in the yard. Berman just touched his wife's arm and she turned her creasing smile on him. Her body was full and soft in the thin, sleeveless summer dress and little drops of perspiration shone on her upper lip. Bright yellow ears of corn were ranged on the table along with baskets of blackberries and crisp summer vegetables wet and still speckled with soil.

"Go cool off, Joe," she said, pushing a little at his arm as though delaying some urgency she saw in his eyes.

When he got his bathing suit on and was walking after Riebold toward the beach, the children descended on him. He picked up Ruthie and Debby. Their bodies were warm and sweaty against him. Ruthie had ice-cream stains around her mouth and she screamed unintelligibly in his ear about some injustice her brother Marvin had done her that day.

Berman turned sternly toward the skinny eight-year-old boy at his heels.

"What did I tell you!"

"She bothered me," the boy said. "They both bother me."

"You're older, you should be gentle with them."

"Put them down, Daddy," Marvin said. "Come on, I'll race you to the beach." He leaned his skinny body forward watching his father with expectant eyes.

"You go run, go ahead. I got to give my little girls a ride. Go on, I'll meet you there." For a moment he thought he saw a flicker of agony in his son's eyes. But then there was just a flat, walled-off expression on the small, lean face. Marvin began to run by himself, his wiry, sticklike legs blurring as he diminished down the street, disappearing finally between the shore-front cottages.

The water was purplish beyond the sand bars. Berman put his daughters down on the ridged mud and started out after Riebold. Off to one side Marvin played with the two Riebold boys. Berman waved to him and Marvin stopped his game to watch his father's passage to the sea but he didn't return the wave. The sky arched a high, deepening blue overhead. He could see the moon like a pale cookie while the sun still scorched his back. And then there was the cool seizure of the water and his own cry of delight as his strength rushed out to each extremity to meet the challenge of the cold water. He splashed and dove and grabbed Riebold's feet from under water. They had a water fight and the water sloshed into their laughing mouths. Riebold looked like a drowning bear in all his thick body hair. Suddenly Berman was hit by a hard, writhing form. A skinny tangle of limbs held his body from behind. He dropped like a stone into the water and plucked the gulping, gasping figure of his son from his back. Then he held him up in the air for a long minute, staring up at the dark, dripping little face with its wild, hilarious, yet insulted eyes.

"You animal, you, you little baboon with a ugly face," he said tenderly. Then he kissed the bony cheek, tasting salt, and looked to see the boy's eyes smile away almost all the insult before he tossed him mightily into the water.

And later he carried his two daughters in his arms while his son sat astride his shoulders, digging occasionally into Berman's neck with his pointy knees as though reminding him of his grievances, of grievances he expected in the future from the father who derived more delight from the awkward helplessness of daughters.

In the wet, mildewy smell of the bathhouse, Berman rubbed his body vigorously. He could hear the supper being set on the big table in the yard, the tinkle of cutlery and glassware, the voices of the two women and the children frolicking hungrily around the temptation of the food.

"Here's pants, Joe," his wife said from the doorway.

Berman pulled her into the dim little room and closed the door. He began caressing her soft, heavy breasts as he pressed his body against hers.

"Joe, Joe," she murmured. "Stop now, please, the children are right outside. Later, later it will be good," she promised, allowing herself one daring touch of his body before slipping teasingly out the door.

"Mary, Mary," he muttered against the closed door, his heart beating in his throat.

"Get dressed, Joe, come out for supper," she said in a mischievous voice against the other side of the wood.

"How can I come out? Now I got to wait a minute. . . . They'll see how my wife teases me. . . ."

He heard her giggle and he shook his head with a big grin on his mouth. His body felt like that of Samson, powerful, white in the gloom of the tiny cubicle. His strength burst out of him. With a sudden cry he smashed his fist into the wooden wall, heard the groaning crack of some of the wood fibers parting. "Watch out for Berman, Berman, Berman," he exulted.

They ate a vast supper, washed it down with quarts of cold beer and iced tea and lemonade. The children all talked at once, addressing their claims, their day's achievements, to the two men at opposite ends of the table. Only Marvin, Berman noticed as he ate, only his son kept watch on his father without words, his large eyes unfathomable in the deceptive shadows of dusk. He loved the boy but there was a barrier between them; never mind whether he himself had erected it or whether it was a mutual project, one of those walls forever built between fathers and sons. He felt impatient at a thousand little actions the boy took and punishment didn't assume the comfortable cycle it followed with his daughters: chastisement, tears, forgiveness, affectionate reinstatement. It was hard for Berman to know his own heart when it came to the boy. He didn't feel the need to reach out and caress, to delight in the softness, as he did with his daughters. A strange, wary little extension of himself, suspect perhaps for being so much like him, privy to his secret impulses. Still there was a feeling of pride, a deep stirring inside when the boy walked through the room. He felt huge and nourishing in the boy's presence, like a tree conscious of its fruit. Ah, well, like a million other things, beyond him . . .

After supper, while the women chattered over the supper

dishes, he and Riebold pitched horseshoes in the deceptive twilight. The clang of iron was a crescendo over the crickets' chirping, the whining, tiny threats of the mosquitoes.

When only the sky was light and the yard was a deep pool of dusk, the women took all the children except Marvin into the house. Ten minutes later, they brought them back to say good night to their fathers. The girls danced around, evading their mothers' hands, wraithlike in their light summer pajamas. Berman stalked them, growling like a great ape so they squealed in delighted terror. Finally he caught them and swept them up in his arms, feeling them wriggle like delicate, sweet-smelling birds as they shrieked their high laughter.

And then, in the quiet, Riebold and Berman argued over their beer; until, in the midst of their laughing and taunting, unaccountably they were on their feet and wrestling while the women giggled and remonstrated with them, calling out warnings, halfhearted disapprovals.

"Joe, Joe, stop that, are you crazy, you'll hurt each other!"

And Riebold's wife cried, "You're a fool, like a big child. Stop, stop, idiots!"

Berman swelled there in the dark yard that was like the bottom of a well whose top was the clear, deep blue of the evening sky. A giant, immensely powerful in the midst of his laughter, he reached with all his might for a strength he felt he would never achieve again in his life. And suddenly, as in a feat brought out of legend, he strained upward and was holding the huge, heavy figure of Riebold over his head, thrusting him at the hollow, star-packed heavens. For a long moment he stood thus in complete silence, feeling the weight of earth and sky on either end as though on the exact median of his life, while the women and the boy watched invisibly in the darkness.

Then Riebold tumbled down on him and there were a few minutes of laughter and hoarse yelling.

But when that was over, Berman knew he still had that moment, would keep it as long as he was blessed with mind and memory. He looked at the pale blur of his son's face and knew it was reproduced there, too, a duplicate copy to insure its preservation. They looked at each other and Berman felt he would have liked to kiss his son's mouth in love. But there were those things between them which would not allow of fruition, so they maintained a sad silence.

In bed he reached for his wife's nakedness with a joy that made him groan. And they grappled to make a hot, powerful, accelerating rhythm. The bed creaked in quiet spasms and the odor of love was mixed with that also spermy scent of cottages near the sea, salt-mixed, moldy, and rank. Until they arched themselves in that terrible ecstatic tension and sighed together down the incline of release.

Then later, on the brink of sleep, Berman thanked God for the obscure blessings, the mysterious joys and near-joys. And after that, alone even from God while his wife slept beside him, he gave his last waking minutes to his son and sadness.

CHAPTER SEVEN   *June, 1956*

Riebold had practically forced him to play cards that night. He sat in a kitchen very much like his own, arranging the jacks and queens and kings. Very faintly he felt the pleasurable excitement of watching a hand form. The smoke from the other men's cigarettes and cigars wound around him as of old. He had been playing with most of them for almost twenty years. The wives played bridge in the living room. They made more noise, used the game more as a vehicle for their conversation. He tried to close the sound of them out of his ears, to sink into the smoke and the cards. A minute spark of rage crackled through his head at the sound of Ethel Riebold's laughter. He wished the kitchen had no doors, was a cosy, isolated chamber he could dwell in for an indeterminate time, fixing only on the little surprises of chance inherent in the cards.

Four aces, ace, king, queen, jack of spades . . . what was the last card . . . a ten of spades. "Three ten," Berman said.

"Count on Yussel," Riebold said with a grin.

"Every time I deal three at a time, Berman gets a hand," said Fox the carpenter. "Well, anyhow, three twenty . . ."

Fox was superstitious about every move in cards. Berman

smiled thinly as he watched the little carpenter tap his cards three times before fanning them out again for another look as though he could thus alter what he had already been dealt.

"Three thirty," Berman said, breathing deeply of the smoky air, his face, as always, indecipherable, professional.

Fox writhed in his chair while Riebold laughed.

"What could he have?" Fox asked himself aloud. "Clubs is dead, he's got no pinochle."

"Try him, Foxy, go on. You ain't gonna get no hint from old Poker-face Berman," Riebold said.

"Ahh, take it, go on, Berman, take it, hang yourself," Fox said in exasperation.

And Berman strode forward in victory, laying his meld before their eyes. "A hundred aces, spades, king, and queen in trump."

He lived in a world of cards and mumbling male voices. After a while he was even able to reduce the sound of the women in the living room to that of a thin, vaguely irritating trickle. He became animated in argument, attacked the play of his partner of a particular game, questioned the wisdom of Riebold's bid, defended himself when he lost a particular hand. Once he called Fox an idiot and then submitted to Riebold's peacemaking. He lived an easy, circumscribed life in those hours, around the formica-topped table with the cigarettes and cigars smoldering in the ash trays, the glasses of soda making wet rings which shone in the bright overhead light. He was a normally peaceful, contented citizen whose only allegiance was to the bright-colored cards and the growing column of scribbled numbers on the score pade. He even laughed aloud once or twice and winked at Riebold over Fox's harassed head. You would have thought he was the same old Berman by the look of him. Indeed, for a while Berman himself was deprived of memory, was limited in his perception to the rosy walls of the kitchen.

Until Fox scraped his chair back from the table and stretched shudderingly.

"I'm pooped," he said. "Hey, it's nearly one o'clock. You took enough of my money, you Berman."

And Berman followed his glance at the clock with a sudden rush of anguish. The smile died on his mouth. The women's voices mounted in the volume that signaled the ending of their game, too, and Berman watched the doorway through which they would come with an expression of dread rounding his eyes.

"Come on, Yussel, I'll run you home," Riebold said gently as he noticed the reinstatement of pain on his partner's face. "Got a lot of work tomorrow, hah?"

Berman felt a stabbing pain in his chest as he stood on the porch before the black windows. They were like empty sockets in a dead face. It made the act of stepping through the doorway actually repulsive, like the obscene contact with a corpse. "I should leave a light," he muttered, trying to ward off a feel of darkness that no lamp could dispel.

He went through the whole house, turning on lights. He imagined the look of the house from outside, the long row of windows on the side presenting a festive brilliance to his neighbor. Perhaps his neighbor thought he was raising Cain now that he was foot-loose. A cruel smile touched one side of his mouth at the idea. "Blondes with whisky, maybe a dope-addict orgy . . ."

In the living room he turned on the television set. He could tell by the music it would be some kind of mystery. There was some hotel in Switzerland, it looked like. He turned one of the lamps off to see better. A murder was committed. No one knew . . . the young man and the young girl were going on one of those European trains . . . someone dropped something on the young girl . . . she was knocked out . . . but she was all right . . . they got on the train . . . that older woman, too. You could see there was going to be trouble. . . .

After a while his body relaxed. He watched the mystery unfold, his eyes rapt on the screen. Watch out . . . uh oh . . . but those two Englishmen . . . they must have seen. . . . Most of him opened up to the pleasurable tension. He sprawled back in the big armchair, his head back, looking down his nose at the picture. But he kept a small, beady-eyed vigilance on the last portal to ease. He kept just enough of himself immersed in pain to avoid that complete involvement that might lead to calling out her name.

He began to get drowsy. The violence of the story took on a soft-edged quality for him. Suddenly, irrelevantly, he remembered his daughter's suggestion about taking in a boarder. Another voice, someone he could call out to without risking that horrid agony of dumbness. Even a stranger . . . anyone . . . tomorrow he would ask around . . . maybe put an ad in the paper. What could he lose? . . . What could *he* lose? . . . Sleep on it . . . Uh oh, that guy's got a gun. . . . Ah, well . . .

September, 1924

Driving into the heat-distorted perspective of the black asphalt road he still couldn't believe the fact of her beside him. She wore a white linen dress with huge buttons running from her shoulder down over the line of her breast, which refused the concealing style the designer had intended.

He felt humble and proud, more than anything incredulous. For three years he had courted her with little apparent success. She was beautiful, "American," intelligent. He had known his limitations. Sometimes she had been provoked into insulting him. "Really, Joe," she had said once when he had taken his whole week's wages to buy her a wrist watch. "It isn't right your giving me such expensive gifts. I don't feel right about it. The fact is that we really aren't suited to each other. We like different things. I don't want you to think that I . . ."

"No, no, no obligation. Money don't mean nothing to me," he had said with a hard smile on his thin, homely face. "Just a little something, don't worry about it."

But he had kept after her with an implacable persistence that had almost seemed to stun her. She was a gay girl who loved parties and dancing, gave enthusiasms to all the frivolous little clichés of the day. One boy almost swept her off her feet after drinking champagne from her shoe. She thought Romance was her mission in life and smiled lovingly on a half-dozen young Arrow-shirt profiles who wore college-fraternity pins enticingly on their lapels. Sometimes she felt an exasperated oppression at the sight of the ugly young greenhorn standing patiently at the side of dance floors, watching her with an intensity that dissolved her flirtatious smiles. His oversize hands hung brutally from his immaculate, expensive jacket sleeves, his fingernails clean but broken and scarred from his work. His clothes were beautiful, costly, but all wrong on him. He looked like a walking investment in something. What? Her? She used to shudder at the way he seemed to seal her in. "I'm not for you, Joe, let's get that straight so you won't be hurt someday."

"Am I asking anything from you, Mary? Don't worry about it. I show you a good time? Okay, so enjoy. You got something else to do sometimes, okay, go ahead. I'm not making claims."

But in a subtle, almost remorseless way he was. It was just that he always was there, an object of her corner vision, a punctuation to her evenings, always just on the periphery of her attention. Sometimes when she was at a dance with someone else, she would see him there with another girl, watching her, serious, humorless, relentless.

Then one night a young halfback from Princeton misinterpreted her coquetry. She found herself splayed out on the grass within earshot of the dance band, with the heavy-shouldered young athlete only inches from making her a fallen woman. "Oh, please, please," she sobbed at the hot touch of his body on her exposed thighs.

And then, without a blare of trumpets, indeed almost noise-lessly, a pair of broken-nailed, powerful hands laid hold of the athlete's shoulders and heaved her attacker into the grass. The halfback rose up in sneering rage, his fists cocked confidently in perfect boxing form against the ugly, skinny young plumber.

But Berman had advanced with his arms at his sides, talking softly, almost affectionately to the Princeton youth. "I'll kill you if I touch you, I'll strangle you to death. I don't know how to box. I'll just tear out your throat." And the football player had retreated into the darkness as though indeed he had looked death in the face.

And later she had trembled with a depth of feeling she had never considered before as Berman said to her, "All I know is I would do everything for you as long as I live and nothing would be too much for me. I know how to suffer; I would suffer any pain for you. This is something terrible for me. I have never felt like this." His big-nosed, pale face showed an agony of awkwardness and strain; his lips were white and looked as hard as bone.

"Do you love me, Joe, is that what you're trying to say?"

"Love?" he said in puzzlement. It was a strange word on his lips. She had heard it come so smoothly, so gracefully from the mouths of former admirers. "Don't you realize? I want you to be my wife. I would give you my whole life, everything."

So, strangely shaken by a nakedness of feeling she had al-ways avoided seeing before, she had reached out to touch his face, really in a pitying gesture. She had been stricken by the sudden shuddering which came over Berman as he dropped his head into her lap and began to cry.

"You'll marry me?" he said in a muffled voice from her lap.

And with the same dazed wideness to her eyes as though a revelation were in the process of continuous unfolding, she nodded first, and then, realizing he couldn't see her nod, answered in a hoarse voice, "Yes, Joe, all right. . . . I guess I must. . . . There's nothing else for me to do. . . ."

And so now they were approaching the limits of New London for their honeymoon, with the smell of gasoline and dusty upholstery from the gleaming Essex in their noses, and the heat, which made an oven of the inside, somehow sealing them in an intimacy that horrified Mary.

Then they were at the seaside hotel where they were to stay and she helped Berman with their belongings, feeling a growing oppression at what she had committed herself to. And Berman sensed it, too. His wonderful elation, which had sustained him through the whole, sparse-worded trip, now seemed to be deflating. Something in her taut, unsmiling face as they followed the hotelkeeper up the stairs told him the whole range of her feelings. She was not proud of the horny-handed, ugly youth, indeed was even shocked and humiliated, as though she had waked in a strange bed with a man she had never seen before. Pity had taken her this far, he realized, and now she was doomed to a grotesquely permanent relationship with him. Well, he didn't blame her, he thought, feeling despair and hurt blacken his vision so much he could barely muster a smile for the proprietor, who told them he hoped they enjoyed their stay there. Who had he been fooling—himself, her?

He looked at her back as she sat on the edge of the one white iron bed in the room. It was a ghastly mistake. What was wrong with him, thinking he could take *her* like any one of the dozen girls he had visited hotel rooms with in his days of bachelorhood. He stood with a suitcase in his hand in the middle of the floor, searching in his mind for some consolation, some apology he could offer her. The sea wind blew the curtains gently into the room with a smell of salt. The setting for his wildly lovely daydream remained, even while the life drained out of it.

"I'll go downstairs and wait . . . if you want to rest maybe . . . wash up. . . ."

She didn't answer but only remained in that motionless pose of dejection on the bed.

"When you're ready, come down. We'll go eat dinner. . . ."

And he closed the door on her there, to walk down the dusty-carpeted hallway. There was a salty, resinous smell to the walls, which were made of narrow, vertical boards stained a nondescript brown. At the head of the stairs he stopped at a little table to touch the sea shells arrayed there in informal decoration. They were fluted and white and seemed to be some sort of declaration of festivity, placed as they were without excuse or reason.

For a long time he stood there, gazing out the little hall window. He could see the beach across the road, the sand darkened by the innumerable pockets of shadow scooped out by the lowered sun. He imagined the feel of it on his feet, warm on the surface but cool underneath, how fine it would have been to walk on it beside her with nothing between them except quiet smiles.

Someone started up the stairs from the floor below. As though in embarrassment at the thought of being seen there alone, he whirled and walked hurriedly back down the hall to their door. For just a moment he hesitated there, then with a deep breath pushed in.

She stood half-bent beside the bed, her arms crossed over her full, naked breasts. Her eyes were wide and held a strange expression, a look both fearful and determined.

"I'm sorry," Berman said. "I didn't think . . . I'll go back downstairs. . . ." He shrugged almost piteously. "We will do whatever you want. . . . We'll talk. . . . I'll let you do anything you want. . . . I won't stop you from going away from me. . . . People make awful mistakes sometimes. . . . I don't blame you. . . . I could see how you feel. I thought it was too good to be true. I bothered and bothered after you. . . . I don't blame you. . . ." He kept his eyes averted from the indescribable brilliance of her white, plump body. "When you're ready, come downstairs. At least we can go to a restaurant and have supper. . . . Maybe we'll talk? Don't worry," he said gently, as though reassuring a child. And with that note of tenderness seeming to lend him a calm, a resignation, he was able to raise his eyes and look serenely on her nakedness. It was as though he set her away from himself.

But as he reached for the door, she said his name.

"Joe."

He turned back to her questioningly.

"I'm yours," she said with a smile.

He blinked for a moment as though a great light had been turned in his eyes. Then he shook his head as though denying the old power of his desire.

"Yes, Joe," she said, her voice trembling but determined. "I'm a foolish girl. . . . Teach me. . . . Show me your love." Her lips showed white around the edges at the ordeal of nakedness. "Come to me, Joe, come to me. . . ."

And it was foolish and awkward at first, with the two of them crying and touching and murmuring little unintelligible words. Berman's clothes resisted both their hands. She bumped her head on the headboard of the bed. Berman became snarled in his trousers. He moaned in exasperation. Ugliness and ludicrousness threatened. She gave a little cry of pain as he rolled against her breast in his struggle to extricate his arms from his shirt. And then, in a moment when he seemed trapped in his undershirt and lay back in miserable defeat, the tears an abomination on his face, she suddenly leaned over him so her large, white breasts grazed his face and she kissed his bared chest. Then she began to laugh, sweetly, happily, as she rested her head there.

Smiling, filled with an ineffable joy, Berman eased his undershirt off. Then he took her very gently and with an ease and grace which awed both of them. So that afterwards they lay entwined and motionless for a long time.

The light outside the window filled with blue and violet and then was dark and moonless. They could hear the ocean booming on the shore and people's voices thin and gay in the coastal air. From a distance came the frail, melodic wail of a calliope and from somewhere behind the house the steady din of crickets like glass beads being shaken. And all of it was rounded and climbing as though shaped by the great bowl of the sky. To Berman it was immensely flattering, as though it were a performance put on for him.

"My God, my God," he said to himself gratefully.

But she heard even his inner voice and turned to him again and they were together again. But this time there seemed little passion in the act; it was more a sort of pledging and a ritual of something which could outlast the burning beginning.

And after that Berman sighed peacefully.

"I'm starving, Joe," she said, holding his coarse, broken-nailed hand to her mouth, kissing even the smooth-polished stump of the missing finger. "We never did go to eat."

Berman laughed softly in the salt-smelling room, suddenly a surer, more gracious man.

"We'll eat and it will be good now. . . ." He turned toward the window where the dark air moved the curtains. "Everything will be good now. . . ."

CHAPTER EIGHT

He opened his eyes to the bland, buzzing channel pattern on the television screen. It was too early for any programs, so there was only the circle with the words CHANNEL 8.

He was still dressed in his clothes of the previous evening, had slept sitting up in the armchair. His neck ached and his body felt stale with an insidious filth. The room was airless, seemed hard to breathe in. Suddenly he was filled with hatred for himself, for the gross body which persisted in that terrible indignity. He loathed filth and decay, had always despised men who let themselves become like animals.

"There's no excuse," he said aloud, staring at the cold, lifeless pattern that greeted him. "Got to clean up a little," he said, heaving himself to his feet. "Particular for a *boarder.*" He said it scornfully but it got him moving.

He took the vacuum cleaner from the dining-room closet and plugged it into the socket in the living room. The harsh, electric whine of the motor made him wince involuntarily even though he knew there was no one's sleep to be concerned about. He had never vacuumed the rugs before and the sound of it unnerved him as though it were a forbidden voice he impersonated, an area he trespassed on.

After the rugs he dusted the furniture and wiped the mirror

77

over the imitation fireplace. And only when he had gone over the entire house did he go into the bathroom to relieve himself and wash off the faint stickiness he felt all over his body.

When Riebold blew the horn for him, Berman went to the door and signaled his partner to come inside. The house resounded to Riebold's voice, seemed to awake, as though it were the first living voice in those rooms. It made Berman think of his solitary weeks there as being a sort of living death, himself something that hovered in a private limbo.

"I tell you what I got on my mind, Leo," he said, waving his partner to a chair. Riebold sat gingerly on the edge of the worn, brocaded seat cushion, respectful of a living room in his work clothes. "You can imagine what I got here, what I'm going through. . . ." Berman waved at the neat, untouched rooms as though that brief gesture could encompass the magnitude of his suffering. "It's very hard to be here by myself. . . ."

"I know, I know, Yussel, I can just imagine," Riebold said pityingly.   •

"All right, no sense in going into that," Berman said with a touch of his usual impatience at sentiment and demonstration. "The thing is I got to do something. Ruthie told me I should take in a boarder. I thought it was crazy at first but things are getting impossible now. I'm going to try to rent one of the bedrooms, probably Marvin's room. I'll try it, I made up my mind. I don't want to talk about whether you think it's a good idea or not. All I want from you—I have no idea about this kind of thing—is how to go about it, what to do."

"A boarder," Riebold echoed, his head cocked speculatively. "I didn't think of it myself, but why not? Sure, it makes sense."

"I already figured that myself," Berman said dryly. "What I want from you is how to go about it. What, do I call up a real-estate agent or what?"

Riebold chuckled, waving his hand disparagingly at Berman's

ignorance. "You're like a babe in the woods, Yussel, you don't know the first thing."

"When you get through enjoying how dumb I am . . ."

"I'm sorry, Yussel, it's just that you're so helpless in some things."

"These things are all new to me," Berman said in a cold, reminding voice.

"Of course, of course, I'm sorry, Yussel." Riebold edged his heavy body farther back on the chair. He felt a little license at his sudden importance to his partner and his face took on a somewhat pompous gravity. "Now, word of mouth is really the best way."

"Word of mouth?"

"Like you let it get around that you want to rent a room, see. So maybe Ruthie tells one of her friends who knows someone or maybe I tell Fox, and he knows a man who lost his wife recently. . . ."

"Fox is a shnook," Berman said, beginning to lose confidence in his friend's knowledge. "And Ruthie, who does she know, all young people who are married."

"No, no, I only mean for instance, not Ruthie and Fox necessary, only for instance."

"If not Ruthie and Fox, who else then?" Berman demanded, standing aggressively in the center of the room. Riebold heaved a little sigh, breathing in forbearance for his sorely tried friend. He looked around at the defiantly clean room and somehow more of the agony of his partner became clear to him. "Anyhow, I'll ask around. But meantime, the best thing for you to do is to call the *Register*."

"The newspaper?"

Riebold nodded. "You ask for the classified."

"The classified," Berman repeated uncertainly.

"It's where they carry the ads for jobs and real estate and rents."

"Oh, yeah, the *classified*. So what do I tell them?"

"You tell them to put in a ad that you got a room for rent."

"It's got to be a single man," Berman said. "How much can I ask? And I don't want no kitchen privilege, just to sleep. He can sit around at night and look at television. How do I tell them that I don't want no drinkers?"

"You just say, 'Single man desires . . .' Oh, cripes, you got a pencil and paper, I'll write it down what you should tell them to put in the ad."

In the kitchen Riebold printed the message with a tiny scoring pencil on the back of a bridge pad. He felt Berman sitting patiently, expectantly, across the table from him as he composed the ad, and the uniqueness of his friend's humility somehow wrung his heart, so he kept his eyes carefully down on the paper as though deep in thought.

" 'SHERMAN AVE. Single man for clean, furnished room in nice, quiet neighborhood. No housekeeping. Furnish references. SPruce 9-1000,' " Berman read. He shook his head in respect for the succinct message. "That says everything, hah?"

"Everything," Riebold answered, unable to resist pride.

"How about the price?"

"When they call, then you tell them. Make it ten dollars a week minimum."

Berman made a little grunting sound.

"What is it?" Riebold asked, concerned about possible defects in his abilities.

"Nothing," Berman said almost dreamily. "Only I was thinking how easy it is to get rid of something—people, rooms . . ."

"Aw, Yussel, don't think about it . . . don't."

"Don't worry about me, Riebold," Berman said with a hard little smile. "This part is nothing. After what I been through, this is like falling off a log."

"Sure, Yussel, sure it is."

"It's the truth, Leo, like falling off . . . a log."

Then they sat there in silence for some time, Berman because he was in another room of his private hell and Riebold because he could see him there but could do nothing about it.

It amazed Berman, the quantity and variety of people who answered his newspaper ad. Then, too, there was a foolish, almost childish sense of power in it for him; that he, who had been living on a sort of dark perimeter in the lonely house, who had wandered the empty streets like a wraith in the early mornings, unable to stir the living people of all the breathing houses, now with the negligible effort of a brief telephone conversation was able to bring them all seeking from *him*. He had to sit on the little flicker of cruelty it brought out in him. With conscious effort, he kept his face and voice bland and objective. He strove for disinterest as he allowed one after another of the strangers into his living room. Seated across from them like some lofty, inscrutable judge, he listened to their aspirations, their wishes, their complaints. Some berated him for letting the cracks appear in the ceiling of his son's room or scolded mildly about the need for painting the front porch. To these people he gave a mocking little smile and told them to "go someplace fancy."

But there were others who wanted exactly what he seemed to offer. Several were university students and these he politely but firmly refused, pointing out that he retired early and didn't wish to be disturbed. One old man with a large head and greenish skin grew very enthusiastic.

"It's just what I've been looking for. I like the location and the fact that it's on a first floor. Oh, you can't imagine how long I've been looking for just a nice, clean place like this," he exulted gratefully, ready to move in. "I got this heart condition and a touch of the sugar diabetes, and I could really relax knowing there was a responsible man around."

And feeling somewhat heartless, Berman had to refuse him.

He couldn't see himself hovering attentively over an old, sick man, and he did not wish to face death again so soon, even a stranger's. "I'm sorry, mister. I had in mind a working man."

"Oh, you don't have to worry about me being solid." The old man chuckled, exposing huge, grotesque false teeth which did a little dance to his merriment. "I'm on retirement from the railroad, solid as the Rock of Gibraltar."

"No, it's not just the money. Just I'd rather have a . . ."

Suddenly the old man's face underwent a remarkable change. The sagging features seemed to collect themselves and his expression came out strong and full of dignity. He even managed to stand straighter as he reached for the doorknob.

"That's all right, you don't have to make excuses. I've been through this before. You don't want to have to watch out for an old, sick man. Well, I don't blame you. Think nothing of it. I got a few more places to try," he said with a little wave of his spotty old hands. "Sorry to trouble you." He went out with that curiously erect posture still intact, but Berman, watching him go down the street from behind the blinds, saw his figure begin to sag as he walked, so that by the time he turned the corner he had shrunk to a tiny, hunched shape that barely looked human.

So by the time the thin, hollow-cheeked young man came, Berman was twitching with a painful anger at his ordeal. His words came out curt and harsh and it seemed he wanted nothing so much as to have it over and done with.

"You want the room, all right, just the way it is, ten dollars a week. Suit yourself."

"I-i-i-it's fine, a-a-a-absolutely fuh-f-f-f-fine," Russel Jones said, shouting the last word finally as though in triumph at having got it out at all.

Berman gave a tiny groan. He shrugged, not caring any more one way or the other. "No kitchen privileges," he warned wearily.

"N-n-n-no, I understand. It's just f-f-f-"

Berman held his hand up to forestall the rest of the struggle. "All right, you can have it," he said. Then, relenting a little at the sight of the timid, dark-shadowed eyes, "You can watch the television whenever you want."

"Oh, I'm so g-g-g-glad to get it. I w-w-work as a wa-waiter down at the hotel and I've been taking a bu-bu-bus all the way from my muh-muh-muh-mother's house in West Haven."

"Well, make yourself at home," Berman said with a frown. "Just make yourself at home." And then in spite of himself he gave vent to a long, harried sigh.

In his bed that night Berman strained to hear the little sounds the young man made over his toilet. It was as though he were looking for the dividends on his efforts. Somehow he was going to get comfort out of having another living creature in that house, he told himself almost defiantly. He lay tensed and alert for the other man's footsteps, nodded with a bleak satisfaction as he went past in the hallway and cast his shadow briefly through Berman's bedroom. He heard the sudden little jingle of some falling coins and the apologetic intake of breath that followed the tiny commotion. There was the click of the light switch and the groan of the bedsprings in his son's room, and for a moment the fleeting impulse of a father's love went through him, only to end in the old morass of grief. He bared his teeth at the ceiling and tried to let his body relent, to let his mind sleep.

For a while there was a silence, more intense, it seemed, than when he was alone in the house. Then there came a steady, rhythmic creaking from the other bedroom, accompanied by the stifled yet clearly audible pants of developing passion. Finally there was a strangled moan, silence again for a moment, and then the low, pillow-muffled sound of weeping.

Berman snarled into the darkness, a sound of mingled compassion, fury, and exasperation. "A real jokester, hah! Got a

lot of tricks up your sleeve for me yet, hah!" he said to his im-
mortal enemy. Then he closed his eyes tight and began groping
for another place, a lost time.

December, 1916

It had snowed just a little during the night, probably sometime
around dawn; the horses' halters and yokes were lightly dusted
with it and the streets had just enough of a fine, powdery snow
to leave footprints. Everything was gray and the air was cold,
with a damp penetration. Looking about at the buildings and
stores made more dark and dingy by the outlining white of the
snow, Berman was surprised at his feeling of exaltation. He
smiled at the cap of snow on a barber pole and the myopic
stare of the barber peering through his steamed window as
though at a blizzard.

What was it, he asked himself, trying to breathe reason into
his mood. Just another morning heading for work with nothing
to look forward to in the hours of the day except hard, cold
work and the steady stream of insults from the anti-Semitic
Irishman who bossed the job. He looked around the grimy, un-
attractive street as though to find some logical excuse for his
feeling of happiness, for that peculiar airiness of spirit. In shop
windows there were little tokens of Christmas and in some of
the narrow front yards he passed, scraggly evergreens were
decorated with baubles of bright-colored glass. It wasn't *his*
holiday, although Hanukkah was also a week away. He thought
briefly of the good, rich smell of his mother's cooking and of
the warmth there would be in his house that night when
relatives came to call and maybe some of his friends came up
to drink glasses of his mother's homemade sweet wine and sit
around one corner of the living room cracking walnuts and
arguing politics until the older folks began shushing and tossing frowns at them.

But why feel so good, he asked himself, ignorant of the blessing of his youth and strength, for he knew only that. Only, he guessed, as though at a brief peek at mystery, there were times when joy awoke in him with a violence that declared itself invulnerable. This morning was one of those times. He felt he could go through all manner of terrors and pain with his joy showing intact at the end. Perhaps it was nothing more than a subtle physiological cycle, which gave him, from time to time, a great, instinctive appreciation for the very flow of blood in his veins. There were times like that morning in which the ability to swing his legs and taste the air seemed aspects of a stupendous endowment, which he acknowledged by smiles or little chuckles, so that people he came in contact with returned his good nature condescendingly, as though they thought him simple-minded. His own voice was a marvel to him, an amazing instrument he had to try even when he had nothing special to say. His mother and his older brother turned frowns on his little spurts of words, which showered on them like spray from an invisible source. Their own pleasures and happinesses were better integrated, were mixed more thoroughly with their grievances. They were always pretty much the same people.

"Hanukkah and Christmas—something, hah?" he had said to their sleepy morning faces, his voice throaty as though a laugh were just beneath. "Big doin's, some of the family coming over, all the Christmas trees for the *goyim*. Oh boy, it's something, I'll tell you." And he would know he was raving even before his brother growled that he was. But Berman knew, too, that his brother was powerless before that awesome vitality, and he only chuckled at his mother's disapproval.

He came up to the huge open trench in the street where a few of the men were already gathered, preparing to minister to the dark wound in the snowy roadway. His teeth sucked the cold, wet air from behind his smile. He had to chuckle at the irritated looks on their pinched faces, and that only made their expression deepen into anger.

"What's so funny, Yid?" the foreman demanded. He had thick, big-pored skin, and his shapeless fighter's nose was perforated and huge like an old potato. "You got a stupid face, you know that!"

"I got what God gave me," Berman said good-naturedly, shrugging and looking at the rest of the men, who seemed to relent, one or two even awarding him smiles in return.

"I got what God gave me," the foreman mocked. "Cut out the bullshit and let's get to work, hah! What do you think this is, Yid, a bank or somethin'? It's quarter to eight. Get your dumb Jew self down in that hole and start diggin'."

"Yessir, Mr. Foreman," Berman said, leaping gracefully down into the slushy trench.

One after another the other men followed, making wet, plopping sounds in the mucky trench bottom. The dirt was heavy with wetness and the throw to the top required a long heave. Before long the men stopped their conversation, putting everything into the great grunts of effort. Only Berman worked with a queer little smile. The foreman walked the length of the trench and back, his frown deepening every time his eyes fell on Berman. From down below almost everything on earth was invisible. Only the sky related to them, gray and shifty, impossible to gauge for depth or distance, so that one moment Berman saw it as an infinite realm of rolling, pearly space, only to feel, in the next moment, that he could reach up and touch it, that indeed it lay on his shoulders with great weight. Along the dark, raw-red edge of the ditch the foreman moved like some strange, menacing indicator, foreshortened and powerful.

Berman tossed him the flat smile as he straightened joyfully against the weight of the heavens, and rage piled up in the bitter, pitted face. Yet silence held, except for the abrasive sound of the shovels, the occasional clinks as they turned aside stones, and the heavy grunting. The dampness encompassed them, coming off the dirt walls of the hole like the wet breath of a great sleeping animal. With each effort, each straining of muscle, Berman's inexplicable joy mounted. Like a silent paean of music the sourceless delight swelled in him. He began singing, in a low monotone, the words of an old Hebrew song.

"Dy, dy, anu, dy, dy, anu, dyanu, dyanu-u . . ."

The foreman's face came alight with threat. He almost seemed to be smiling in relief as though Berman had given him something he had been looking for.

"Cut out them Jew songs, Yid. And cut out that standing up to rest every five minutes. You're getting me mad, Yid." He squatted down on the lip of the trench to be closer to Berman, and his eyes shone with a gay war light. "Standin' there with that crappy grin on yer crappy Jew face . . . I'm gettin' fed up with you, Yid."

"I'm getting fed up with you, too," Berman said, matching the fierce gaiety of the Irishman. And then, deliberately, with his eyes on the potato nose just a few feet away, he began again to sing, *"Dy, dy, anu, dy, dy, anu . . ."* standing erect so it came out like some ancient war cry while all around him the other men stopped to lean on their shovels under the infinite height of the gray sky. The half-exposed pipe gleamed rustily in its wetness and the puddles in the mud reflected the pale light like flat chips of glass. A little wind blew tiny particles of wet snow off the top of the trench and Berman's face shone and tightened with its cold touch as he sang to the brooding, vital face over him.

"Dyanu, dyanu-u-u . . ."

"Your mother's a whore, Yid," the Irishman said, with a grin for the imminence of combat. And oddly Berman knew the foreman had lost his malevolence, that the fantastic insult was a sort of tribute, a ritual gesture toward battle. For the first time the Irishman was acknowledging him an equal, and he knew a perverse affection for the brutal-faced man, because he himself was a battler deep inside, under the traditional repugnance for violence that Jews have.

So his own smile widened in abandon for a moment before he lunged for the man's feet and pulled them toward him. The heavy figure crashed into him and they fell into the soft, wet bottom of the trench. For a moment he was shocked at the dangerous strength of the embracing arms, the prodigious weight. They rolled silently in the mud while a low, awed murmur went up among the watching men. Berman found his face in the thick, watery mud. His eyes saw nothing and his mouth opened to the viscous atmosphere of earth and water. The powerful arms forced his ribs in on his lungs and for a moment he thought he would drown there in that viewless pit to the sound of splashing limbs and the low calls of encouragement from an invisible audience; until, with a spasm of desperate strength, he threw his own body into a spin and saw the colorless sky through his dirt-clogged lashes. But the massive arms continued the terrible oppression and blackness began filling the sky, too, as his brain died for air. He brought his head forward until his chin touched his chest, then snapped it back suddenly to crack with dull impact on the face of his opponent. And the arms opened to the snarl of pain so that Berman could spin his body over and over away from the squeezing arms. Then they were on their knees a few feet apart, each staring in amazement at the mud-covered visage of the other.

"C'mon, kike," the foreman said in a thick, hoarse voice, as though he, too, had swallowed some of the mud. And Berman, with the gritty edge to his teeth, smiled his slumberous Yiddish curses and rose to his feet.

The foreman rushed him but Berman had time to bring up a punch of half-strength which put the heavier man into a halt just out of reach. Now he saw the size and great advantage in weight of his opponent as though for the first time, and he seized a hand-size rock from the ground near his feet. At that, the foreman, an old shillalagh fighter, gave a chuckle of pleasure and came up with a small Stillson wrench from out of nowhere.

"Oho, Yid," he cried, finding new delights in his opponent at every turn.

"Yes," Berman answered in acknowledgment as he swung his rock-laden hand. He met the thick shoulder of the Irishman, who bellowed his pain yet immediately swung his wrench in an expert counterblow which caught Berman on the lower chest with a crunching sound of breaking ribs. And Berman's gurgle of pain came out like a chuckle for the terrible game they played. He pushed the rock straight out in a spasmodic jab. It met the Irishman's face dead center and left a welter of blood mingled with the mud on the broken features.

The foreman wiped at his ruined mouth, looked at the undecipherable smear on his hand, and then lunged too suddenly for Berman to parry. The first blow caught Berman over the ear and knocked him down beside the half-exposed pipe. Then, as he felt his consciousness fade, the second blow, right after, crushed his hand against the cold pipe.

He smiled at the strangeness of not feeling that blow. Then he lay back to face the gray sky, and passed out.

He opened his eyes three days later. He was in his bedroom and there was a smell of raisins and chicken fat in his nostrils. Three of his friends ranged the wall shyly; a smile passed from one to another of them at the sight of his opened eyes. His mother came into the room, severe with her gray hair back in an iron-hard bun. Steam rose from her hands and as she drew close he saw she carried a bowl of soup for him.

"It's a party?" he queried brightly, his voice hoarse from disuse. "All my friends, dinner in bed . . . How come . . . just for this?" he said, touching the thickness of bandage on his head and glancing up toward it with a ludicrous expression. And then, as he lowered his hand, he saw the peculiar bandaging, in which he was unable to account for all the fingers.

"Misery, torturer, it's not enough, the aggravation you give me?" his mother said. "Oh, don't worry, you'll drive me to my grave soon enough. Go, joke that you only have a small hole in your head, that you only lost one finger. . . ."

Berman looked at his finger, or where his finger had been. Then he looked up at the faces of his friends, who looked away uncomfortably in anticipation of his shock. But he only began a broad grin, which widened and widened until it seemed his cheeks would split. His mother glanced worriedly toward the door, where his elder brother stood behind his thin, old-looking face.

"It's affected his head," his brother said solemnly.

Berman concurred, nodding the heavy weight of bandages and holding the bandaged stump up in the air.

"It's affected my head and my hand, too," he said in a strangled voice. "But you should see the other guy." Then he began to laugh, holding his hand to his head as though to keep it from shattering over the violence of his mirth.

And one by one, a little timidly in fear of the mother's disapproval, his friends began to laugh, too—stifled, mouth-covered laughs at first, until, caught by the irrepressible merriment of the patient, they began bellowing, with helpless shrugs for the mother and the frowning brother. And the room seemed to pulse and breathe with the sound until there was room for nothing else, so the mother began to smile angrily, then shake furtively for a moment. Then, defeated, she squealed and waved her condemnation at the folly of it. Even the older brother went through an elaborate series of winces and face-making, caught himself, and, horrified at his own weakness, whirled and hurried out of sight.

"Oh, you Berman," the short, wiry boy with the square head howled.

"Eeee-eee-eeeey-Yussel," shouted the husky youth named Riebold. "Such a time to laugh!"

"Mashuginah, insane, insane," Berman's mother protested, her apron up over her mouth. "Stop, stop before you hurt . . ." But she was engulfed in the laughter and went out defeated, her apron over her head as though in shame.

The friends writhed, hit each other, dropped into chairs, only to spring up again as though stung. And all the time Berman lay with the bandaged hand up to the bandaged head as though keeping the symbol of his peculiar delight before them, while he shook silently, tears streaming from his eyes, which he kept closed. His head throbbed to his shaking but he could not stop any more than his friends, who had become so susceptible because they had expected sorrow and pain and had been unnerved by relief when they found something altogether different.

One by one they emptied themselves of the hysteria and sank down on chairs, wiping their eyes and shaking out the little residues of mirth. Berman, too, lowered his hand weakly at last and began dabbing at his face with the sheet.

"Such a hero," Riebold said. "What's a finger to Berman!"

"Even the head is nothing to him," the small, wiry boy, whose name was Fox, cackled.

"Even the head," the third youth, a fat boy named Bonoff, echoed as though it were an example of the utmost wit.

"How's the Irisher?" Berman asked.

"Uglier than before," Fox said.

"He sent you a get-well card," Riebold said.

And they laughed at that again, not quite so hard as before, but fondly rather, as though in reminiscence of the uproarious joviality.

And Berman looked at his spirit to find his joy in one piece as he had known it would be, or maybe even greater now that it had been tried. His heart sang with that mysterious exaltation that had no basis in reason, no foundation of motive or history. There in the green-painted room with the cracks painted over like healed scars, among his friends and the cherished bric-a-brac his mother had brought from Russia with all the other worthless heirlooms, with the cold New England air intolerant against the puttied panes, in a world of common pain, present in his body and anticipated in his mind, he held to that odd transcendence, that bodiless flame both fragile and mighty which held him in a solitude he would not relinquish for all its loneliness.

His mother came in with a tray that held a bottle of wine and various-shaped glasses and a plate of her *kichel,* which melted on the tongue with the delicacy of a snowflake. So they sat around the bed, sipping the sweet wine, munching, talking, chuckling, toasting their fallen friend, who sat up now against his pillows like a king. Even his older brother came in to spread cigar smoke over the other warm smells. The lamp shone orange through the colored-glass shade, glinting on the lately displaced gas jets and making the smoke into floating amber yarn. The mother sat beside Bonoff and let herself be consoled, nodding to his murmured cheer, smiling a little as though half-convinced now that pain and worry were vanquished for the while.

But later, alone in the room which was suddenly invaded by moonlight as the clouds parted, Berman felt pain, strong and living in his head and where his finger had been, and he was swollen with the joy of it, burned with recognition, as though it were the overpowering evidence, irrefutable, of some towering presence.

CHAPTER NINE

"Russel," Berman said, lifting his upper lip in a grimace of awkwardness. The name went off his tongue with an alien, wooden sound. "Russel, that's no kind of supper, a lettuce sandwich. What are you, a rabbit, that you can live on lettuce?" He spoke wearily; he was tired of pitying the hollow-eyed young man after a week of seeing him creep around the rooms solicitously, after watching him studiously avoid the sight of Berman's own modest suppers.

"Oh, that's all r-r-right, Mr. B-Berman. You'd be-be-be huh surprised how nourish-shing it is. . . . I-eeeee-eee get along just f-f-fine. . . ."

And Berman—thinking, Christ, you need more strength for just your shenanigans in bed than that lettuce could give you—growled impatiently, "Take some of this meat and put it on. Go ahead, there's plenty."

"Aw, now, Mr. B-B-Berman . . ."

"Take it, I say," Berman snapped, watching the pale, embarrassed smile of the young man as he obeyed, taking two thin slices of the browned meat and shrugging as though intimating he was just doing it to please his landlord. "Tell me, Russel," Berman said in a flat, merciless voice as the man's

93

starving mouth bit with delicate restraint into the now heartier sandwich, "what do you do with yourself when you're not waiting on tables down the hotel? Do you got any social life, go out with girls, play pool, go to the movies? I'm not trying to be nosy, I never did mind anybody's business but my own. But it seems to me you don't make enough money to keep yourself together. Why did you move out of your mother's house? Wouldn't it be easier living at home?"

"Well, n-n-now, Mr. Berman," Russel said from a full mouth that now seemed to be gagging him. "I th-th-think you are being a little per— huh huh personal. You've been very n-nice, I don't want to sound disrespectful, but yuhhhh-hh-hh . . ." His mouth held the shape of his intention, his lips paralyzed around a painful silence he couldn't break.

Berman stared at him bleakly; he had reached a point where he could put himself beyond pity. Suffer enough pain and you are capable of many transgressions against your own nature. You become more realistic, more efficient in removing irritations, for you seem to live in a different world. Like the soldier who in civil life is gentle and tender of all forms of life and in the stress of battle can sometimes kill a human being with hardly a tremor of distaste, Berman had reached a weariness of spirit that made him capable of quick, crippling blows.

"Russel, the truth is I can't stand to see you dragging around half-dead. Another thing bothers me is your jerking off in bed at night. Understand I don't condemn you or anybody. People should do what they want, okay. But I had enough aggravation these last few months; I'm having enough trouble trying to get through it as it is. All you're doing is depressing me some more. I figured someone else in the house would make it easier. This sounds mean, nasty, I know. All my life I been the kind of person who hated to hurt people's feelings. Ten years ago I would have said it nicer, made up some excuses that wouldn't have embarrassed you. Thing is I got no patience for that any more. You'll have to try and forgive me, Russel. I just can't stand to live with someone as miserable as me."

He sat back in his chair and his furrowed, big-nosed face behind the glasses held nothing you could see.

Russel looked down at the sandwich with a perplexed expression as though he had bitten on something hard. He had to nod his head once or twice to get the mouthful down. Then several spasmodic smiles spread his mouth the way an electric shock might bring involuntary muscularity into play.

"I cer-cer-certainly think y-y-you-ooo . . ." He shook his head violently—whether in impassioned negation or just to clear his crippled vocal cords, Berman couldn't tell. "That's an awful thing to accuse m-m-m-meee . . . You're making me out some per-err-pervert or sommm . . . or something. I am sh-hh . . ." He shrugged as a bitter, condescending smile tried itself on his soft mouth. "Well, you can thh-hhh-hh-think what you w-want, Mr. Berman, but I certainly w-w-will not burden you w-w— huh huh my huh . . ." His stretched-open mouth revealed the remains of the meat sandwich around his tiny, immature teeth. Suddenly his eyes stretched open so wide it seemed the membrane split and they overflowed. He began to make little coughing sounds, which Berman figured to be sobs. Then he began to cry with his eyes open just as wide, gazing with a sort of horror at Berman as though the older man were a grotesque trick mirror that gave him back his image in horrible ugliness.

And Berman sat through it without remonstrance or impatience, feeling he owed himself that much discomfort as some sort of payment. The kitchen was getting dark around the two of them but it was a negligible sort of darkness, a lack of light too trivial compared to that which each of them held in himself. Russel began nodding in time with his sobbing, an agonized sound, as though his soul were shaking itself loose. His thin hands kneaded a piece of the sandwich bread so it seemed the rest of his body was not concerned, was only waiting patiently for the painful sound to end so it could get back to doing some of the feeble exercises its master demanded of it. And Berman, too, was patient, though aging in the melancholy sound of the younger man's weeping. He seemed to have put himself several centuries farther from all the life he had lived up till then. He felt almost a sense of drying in his heart and body. He wondered if the remaining hair on his head was losing pigmentation, imagined looking in the mirror afterwards to find his hair white, his face creased and ancient.

Finally Russel got up, the plate in his hand as he peered uncertainly through the dimness toward Berman.

"Leave it. I'll clean up . . . after . . ."

Russel nodded, took a deep breath, and sighed.

"I'll just get my things together."

"No hurry, Russel," Berman said.

"No, I think it would be better if I left as soon as possible under the circumstances. I won't be more than ten minutes, Mr. Berman."

Then he must have sensed the tiny smile on Berman's face, for the light was not enough for him to have seen it.

"Why are you smiling, Mr. Berman? Was there something funny?"

"No, just that I never heard you say so much without a single stutter," Berman said.

Russel smiled wryly, yet with a peculiar grace and charm that Berman could see in spite of the darkness.

"There are times with me . . ."

And Berman nodded in appreciation of the lovely mystery of the phrase, as though at the sight of a long, brief opening which revealed the unrecognizable treasure of the pathetic man.

Louis Kivarnik was no Russel, Berman thought at the sight of the short, stocky man in the expensive silk suit. He radiated assurance and sensuous satisfaction in his dark, fleshy face, and his black eyes were shrewdly adaptable to the nature of the customer.

"You got a nice, quiet place here, Berman. Just the kind of deal I had in mind. I'm on the road two weeks out of the month and I do my big livin' then. Just want a peaceful place to rest up when I'm in town. That friggin' hotel is a nut house and I need my beauty sleep. I need somethin', cause I'm sure no beauty, hah, hah!" He dug Berman's arm intimately. "No, but serious, Berman, I ain't gettin' any younger, pushin' fifty. Them chippies startin' to wear me out. Gotta live quiet at least half the month, hah! You know how it is when the ol' pecker ain't what it used to be, hah, hah! No joke, hah!"

"No joke," Berman agreed, straight-faced. "The room is twelve dollars a week without housekeeping."

"Perfect, lead me to it, my friend. This old chippy-chaser is plain pooped. I run down from Troy last night, left two years of strength up there. Some town, Troy. You ever cover that town, Berman? I got a feeling you was a hot rock in your time, hah, hah!" He prodded Berman's ribs with a surprisingly sharp elbow, inviting some naughty reminiscence from the expressionless face of this man who looked old and juiceless, as though he had never known pleasure or passion.

"I have stayed pretty much in this town only for many years," Berman answered civilly. "I have lost my wife recently, so . . ."

"Ah, that's too bad, too bad, sorry to hear that," Kivarnik said with a momentary assumption of solemnity. Then, that obligation fulfilled, his dark, sleek face fattened with a smile. "But, you got a life to live. Maybe you'll want to have a little fun now. Any time old Louis Kivarnik can be of service . . . If there's anything I'm an authority on besides kids' clothes, it's in the science of havin' a good time. Name it, I got it— places to eat, to drink, to screw. Believe me. Whenever you're ready . . ."

"Yeh, sure, when I'm ready," Berman replied flatly as he

turned away and began leading his new tenant to his son's former room.

He probably could have borne the sloppiness of Louis Kivarnik if that had been all. For one thing, the terrible cleanliness of the house, which he had maintained as though by compulsion, had cast him into a strange sense of limbo where he looked at the familiar gleam of dusted tables and polished chairs and lived an awful dream in which he was constantly rediscovering his bereavement with great surprise. There was no question about the metamorphosis the rooms underwent with Louis Kivarnik there. Ash trays, many of them virginal through all the years of two nonsmokers, were loaded with blackish-brown cigar butts, which often overflowed onto the table like turds from a herd of animals. Glasses perched on every level and the sticky rings were on table and mantel in the living room. Bits of cellophane from the cigars were between all the seat cushions on the couch, and empty matchbooks were likely to be lying spent beside the armchairs or on the bubbled shellac of the television set, where matches had been carelessly dropped while still hot. Berman realized there was no point to keeping up with the housecleaning, so clumps of gray-white dust accumulated like tumbleweed under all the beds. The bathroom shelf was sticky with spilled hair lotion and shampoo. Berman told himself he didn't care one way or the other.

But then Kivarnik began tacking up the nudes. "Art studies —I like to be surrounded with beauty," he said to Berman. And day by day Berman let his outrage accumulate at the sight of his skinny, unfinished son in the A.Z.A. sweat shirt, holding up the fish as though eternally soliciting his father's praise, surrounded by the simpering, leering women with their glossy, obscene poses of invitation. Had Marvin ever known a woman, he wondered. Or if he had, was it only the professional embraces of such as these? It began to obsess him, the circling images around the child's blurry face. As though they were trying to taunt the boy, as though Kivarnik, with his soiled underwear under the expensive white-on-white shirts, were torturing the spirit of his son, or more likely—as an agent of the unseen enemy—himself.

Oh, the man was friendly enough, Berman realized. In his fashion he even put himself out to be pleasant to his taciturn landlord. There were moments when Berman could see the two of them there with an objective and calm view, and he could see the peculiar old stranger he had become and the harmless good nature of his tenant. But mostly he *was* the old stranger and could see only the repulsive dirtiness of the gaudy man who lived in his son's room.

There were grease marks from Louis Kivarnik's vaselined hair on the dainty floral wallpaper over the spare day bed, and the side of the polished bed was deeply marked from the man's habit of striking matches there when he smoked.

"Berman," he said one night, when the smell of flowers came stifling from outside, "why don't you put on some fancy duds and come with old Louis tonight? I got a couple nice drinkin' companions just dyin' for a night on the town."

Berman stood in the doorway of the room, still in his greasy work clothes. Something irresistible had made him creep up to the doorway the way he used to do. It was as though for a moment he had really expected to hear the light, feminine tinkle of the girls' voices, sounding all the more delicate and precious to him for the heaviness of the sweat and weariness on his body. And there had come first the rank odor of the dead cigars, followed by the brassy bellow of Kivarnik's voice as he stood knotting an extravagant red-and-gold tie before the mirror.

Perhaps it was just that terrible wound of disappointment, which certainly wasn't the short, dark man's fault. But added to the days of physical violation he had endured in the careless habits of the man, it detonated his rage, gave him a welcome enemy in lieu of that one he knew he could never come to grips with.

"Get out, Kivarnik," he said through clenched teeth.

"Five minutes. Just got to finish sprucing up. You got to be a little extra careful with yer appearance at my age," Kivarnik said blithely, cocking his head as he surveyed the pleasing contrast of the snowy shirt under his rich, brown face. "Sure you won't come along, Berman? Do you good to get out of these crummy rooms and have a few laughs. Serious, Berman," he said, turning a sincerely concerned expression on the motionless figure in the doorway. "I don't like to see a guy just sit and go to pot like you're doing. You ain't that old yet you gotta lay down and die. Come on, live a little. You'll be dead long enough."

"I want you should take all your fancy clothes, your cigars, your dirty pictures on my walls, and I want you to get out of this house in five minutes." He stood, slightly hunched, heavied with age and suffering, staring through the horn-rimmed glasses that were flecked with spots of dirt and dried dust from the trench he had worked in all that afternoon.

"What the hell's come over you?" Kivarnik asked with genuine surprise. "What's the matter? You don't feel good, what?"

"Don't give me any talk, just get out. I'm sick of your filth," Berman said in a dull, menacing voice.

The acting went out of Kivarnik's face; the wheedling humor was replaced by the hard, knowledgeable expression that had been there all along.

"I don't know what kind of a bug you got up your ass," Louis Kivarnik said in a low snarl. He was no Russel Jones, no old pensioner begging for a quiet corner to die in. The hard salesman's armor was revealed in his manner, and you could see that the showy clothes were no indication of softness but only the uniform of his tough trade. "I don't like to be talked to like that, Buster. I make allowances you're a little screwed up hanging around this house, with losing yer old lady and all, but don't talk tough with me."

"Are you getting out?" Berman said almost wearily from the doorway, looking no match in spirit for the other man, with his stooped body in the shapeless, dirty work clothes.

The weariness must have encouraged the short, heavy man. His eyes narrowed and he advanced toward Berman.

"First place, you tell me decent you want me to leave. This crummy place is no great attraction. 'Sides, you're startin' to depress me, if you want the truth. And second, I'm paid up till the end of the week. Tomorrow I'll get me a place downtown, so relax, don't get your balls in a uproar." He stood with his fat, dark hands confidently on his hips, staring condescendingly at his landlord's glasses; they reflected the evening light, and he couldn't see the savagery in Berman's eyes.

"God help you, you fool," Berman snarled regretfully as he seized Kivarnik with his great, soiled hands, crumpling the starched whiteness. He jammed him viciously against the door and Kivarnik's head thudded heavily against the wood. Then he began shaking him violently, too fast for Kivarnik's head to find the rhythm, so it wobbled erratically, striking the door again and again. All the expression faded from Kivarnik's face; he seemed to pale under the dark surface of his skin, and when expression returned it was with a look of astonishment too severe even for terror.

"I'll go, I'll go." Kivarnik panted. "Stop, stop, you'll kill me," he cried, his eyes streaming though he wasn't crying. Then Kivarnik began moaning, and the shaking gave the sound vibrato. All this might have seemed some peculiar performance between the two men, what with the moaning, toneless note and the uncertain percussion of the head striking the door. And

Berman's face was blank and hidden behind the streaked glasses, Berman himself silent except for the great sound of his breathing.

Finally he released Kivarnik and turned abruptly to walk out of the room and down the long hall to the bathroom doorway, where he stood gasping for breath, hearing the sounds of drawers opening and closing and hangers rattling in the closet. He heard the leather heels walk out of the bedroom, stand for a moment in the hallway as though in uncertainty. Then a little sigh started the footsteps toward the front of the house, through the kitchen, until the carpeting in the two front rooms muffled them. Berman heard the front door close almost delicately, as if Kivarnik were concerned about waking someone behind him in the house. Then there was the silence again, and Berman's own rapid breathing suddenly seemed muffled as though by the intensity of his solitude.

On the wide, dented bed that night he was sure he didn't sleep. From time to time he was aware of the familiar shapes of the furniture and the guardian outlines of the bed lamp, bulbless on the little table beside his bed. Yet in between those dissuading reminders of the time and who he was now, he had vivid, detailed visions that made his face writhe in the darkness in a constant gamut of expression, ranging from the brightest joy to the deepest pain, from the almost brainless look of love to the terrible spastic countenance of hatred. Kivarnik would never have recognized his wooden-faced landlord in the struggling man who lay on his misshapen bed alone in the dark.

October, 1915

Trying to keep his lips from moving too obviously, Berman whispered a prayer of thanksgiving. His eyes watered with gratitude for the sight of his older brother moving through the clear sunlight toward them. Beside him, anchored dutifully to her pile of belongings, his mother muttered her older son's name over and over. "Jacob, Jacob, Jacob, Jacob, Jacob. . . ." She had not seen him for three years and to her simple heart the distance of oceans and of time had made him seem lost to her, so there was something of marvel in her chanting of his name, as though he had come back from the dead.

The autumn day was immense. Blue sky etched the fantastic towers of the strange city and it seemed to Berman that its province extended to infinite heights. The water made little splashing sounds behind him and even the great ship they had just left seemed to rock frivolously on the little waves of the harbor, like a heavy old woman who forgets her age and bulk to try a few steps of a girlhood dance. Crates were ranged the length of the dock and there were pale puddles scattered across the dark wood they stood on. Some babies cried in their mothers' arms, tiny, thin sounds in the huge, open place. The gulls were louder, cawing like peddlers over the oil-rainbowed waters. And there were the hootings of the tugboats as well as the grinding, squealing noise of industry from the busy winches still unloading cargo. Berman felt an inward trembling at the very size he sensed in the city.

"Jacob, Jacob, here, here," he called, adding his voice to his mother's and remarking at the same time how shallow and small his voice sounded.

And then there was a confusion of embraces and calling of names among the three of them. They took turns kissing and hugging each other, so that Berman found himself embracing and kissing his mother as though he hadn't seen her for a long time himself.

"Mama, how are you, I'm so glad to see you . . . you have no idea. And look, look at the size of him, Yussel, Yussel. . . ."

"He was sick the whole way over," the mother said as though that might have had something to do with Berman's size.

"But now you're here, that's the important thing."

And Berman and his mother agreed heartily that that really was the important thing, laughing and crying there in the brilliant, salty sunshine with the babbling voices of the other immigrants all around them, the thin, puzzled sounds of babies crying and the gulls slipping along the invisible channels of the air trailing their own raucous excitement.

The older brother wore the attitude of a blasé American, after his own emotions had eased down. With a lordly air he pointed out the wonders of trolley cars and automobiles as they walked the crowded streets.

"So many people," the mother said. "Where do they all come from? Is it a market day?"

"Oh, Mama." The older brother laughed. "It's always this way. This is New York, the biggest city in the world."

And Berman, struggling along a short distance behind with the load of belongings, nodded a little smugly to himself as his feeling of size was confirmed.

"Is this where we will live?" the mother asked worriedly. "In all this? Is this where you have lived these years?"

And the older brother laughed again as he put his arm reassuringly over his mother's shoulders. "No, no, Mama, we have to take a train to where we live. Our city is called New Haven, a smaller city."

So it was that when the October sunshine was low and golden, the mother peered from the train window with a tiny smile on her mouth.

"Why, it looks something like Kiev," she said happily. "No more or less."

Later, when the lights of their first-floor flat in the large four-family house fell on the sparse grass of the yard, Berman stood by himself gazing at the sparkling stars and sniffing at the odors of fallen grapes and burned leaves. The lights of other houses twinkled through the trees all around him, teasing him like so many bright eyes, with mystery and promise and the goodness of life.

He took a deep breath of the American air; then, looking furtively around to make sure no one was watching, as though he sensed the need for a new decorum in his worship, he began the familiar words as he rocked back and forth on his feet.

"Baruch atah Adonoi elohanu . . ."

Guiltily he felt the presence of a smile on his lips as he intoned the sacred words. But there was no help for it, he realized. Somehow he knew the smile was as big as the years and he could not see the end of it from there. So he went on with his low prayer, rocking as though with the force of the breeze, his eyes closed ecstatically, and smiling, smiling all the while.

CHAPTER TEN

He awakened with the strange shape of a smile on his mouth and for a moment he lay there holding it wistfully, wishing for the old fantasy of happiness. Outside there was the rosy glow of early morning. One cricket made a subdued buzzing, anticipating the heat.

Stiffening his body for reality he swung his legs to the floor, studied their hairless length for a moment, and then almost absently, in murmured Yiddish, wished the black cholera on the world.

He dressed with his eyes semiblind on the window, which opened on a brilliant summer day already redolent with sun-warmed smells of soil and flowers. The worn, dirty work shirt encased his body clammily; as he stood in his doom of loneliness, it gave him the feeling that his torture was something he donned with his own will, and it puzzled him, for he could find no sense to this.

In the kitchen he sat, sipping the hot instant coffee. He had learned the proper proportions and had come to like it just as much as coffee made in a percolator. For a while he had resented the ease, the lack of ceremony in making coffee in a cup, but now he was beyond ritual, looked only for simple,
106

thoughtless ways, unmemorable methods of getting from one night to the next.

While he waited for Riebold, he paced the rooms, trying to hold down a feeling of violence. He held his hands behind him as he walked, clenching and unclenching them as he scanned the tiny fragilities collected by his wife over the years. There was a china shepherdess she had bought on an auto trip in 1936. He remembered vividly the little gift shop somewhere in Massachusetts and the almost bald woman with the horse-like face who had said, "It's genuine Meissen," and how coldly she had received his little retort, "Maybe Bubba Meissen." Mary had laughed and scolded him, apologizing to the woman at the same time. And that plate with the blue sailboat on it, cracked almost invisibly where she had expertly repaired it. She could fix things, little injuries to things and people. How many times had she lowered the swelling angers that came between his son Marvin and himself. Count the doting consolations she had lavished on all their injured prides—his own, the girls', Marvin's.

His hands jerked apart. He grabbed the plate and began very slowly to exert his powerful hands on its delicate surface. For a moment it seemed to tremble as though capable of pain, then it cracked with a small, abrupt, and dry sound.

Riebold's horn sounded outside as Berman stared in amazement at the broken plate. The break was new; where she had cemented it the bond was strong and untouched. With a bland face he threw the two pieces hard against the wall and went to the front door. He stood for a moment with his hand on the knob, listening for something he had no hope of hearing. Then he went out into the lively air.

"I heard something break," Riebold said curiously.

"You heard it so it must have happened," Berman said flatly. Then he sat back in the truck and waited for Riebold to start driving.

All day long it seemed he was going up and down stairs. They were working on a fourth floor and he shouldered lengths of pipe from the truck and carried them up the flights of stairs, remembering how easily he had once done that sort of thing. The heat became intense by late morning and he began to see flashing lights before his eyes. The sweat ran salty into his eyes and his legs began to ache behind the knees. He had to crawl into the narrow space beneath the roof, where he barely had room to work the small wrench on the pipe. The torrid air pressed on him and intensified the odors of tar paper and the dirty, unrecognizable things that had gathered in that confined corner. Mice ran over his legs and the slatted sunshine from a tiny louvered ventilator made white bars on his dark hands. The very flesh on his bones was aged, seemed nailed to the rough flooring, and his heavy breathing was thunderous. He worked with the pipe just inches from his eyes and soon his vision lost focus, and it was as though he worked in a fiery fog. Pain started at the back of his head and gradually scraped forward. He began to curse, not violently but with a regular, low rhythm that became a sort of comforting litany—just so that malevolent mightiness could see and hear that he, Berman, knew what he was being subjected to.

When Riebold dropped him off that night, he waited until he was inside the house to let his body go slack. He slumped in a chair and took great gulps of air. The closed-in coolness of the house chilled him. For a few minutes he felt nauseated, thought he might vomit right on the living-room rug. Finally the nausea passed and with a grunt he raised himself from the chair and walked slowly to the bathroom.

When he was cleaned and dressed only in a fresh pair of undershorts, he went into the kitchen and stood before his small larder of canned food. Listlessly he forced himself to read off their labels, as though that might help him make a decision. He really felt no hunger but realized he needed food after his daily fast.

"Campbell's Tomato Soup, Heinz Oven-Baked Beans, Bumble Bee Brand Tuna, King Oscar Norwegian Sardines, Del Monte Pineapple, Chunk Style . . ."

He never remembered afterward whether or not he came to a decision then. All he knew was a sudden darkening before his eyes, a reeling, the distant sensation of his head striking hardness, and then nothing.

When he opened his eyes he was on a gigantic turntable, which gradually slowed down so he could see the lined terrain of a dry, yellow desert. He felt an astonishing agony; rather, he was one body of single torment. Yet there was no sense of beginning and ending that actual pain has. There was just the barren kitchen ceiling and that incredible, unidentifiable suffering. He felt the awful giddiness one has in a dream of endless space. Eternity beckoned invisibly with a threat of everlasting falling. His life, his memory of people and things, was a tiny dancing mote, a fantastically foolish thing. The minute image of loved faces, the microscopic dream of griefs and losses, lost shape and dwindled to the size of the disordered flitting shapes in his head. Beyond terror, too small to contain the immensity of emptiness, he searched for his voice to cry out.

And in his groping he found outrage, a fury for the reduction of all his strivings.

"Oh, no," he cried as he pushed his body up to a sitting position. "You're not dealing with a timid man. Not so easy . . . I'm Berman!"

Then he was somehow on his feet, shaky but whole, still existent. There was only the ache at the back of his head where he had struck the floor, and the weakness of his body.

Furiously he opened several cans of fish and began eating with his fingers right from the tin. By degrees the food began to calm him. His balance seemed less precarious, his strength came back to his legs and arms. He chewed without relish, conscientiously, intently, dedicated to nourishing himself as though just that would be an expression of defiance. His jaws worked like a beast's as he stared at the windows. The oil from the fish coated his lips and chin, and his fingers were slippery with it.

After he had devoured the contents of three cans, he reached for the bottle of whisky. It slipped in his greasy hands and he caught it just in time. He tilted the bottle up to his mouth, took five or six long swallows, then set the bottle down to feel the animation and warmth dart from his stomach out to his limbs. Finally he took a deep breath and let it out slowly. His anger became less desperate, more vital and strong.

"Come on, come on," he said with a tough, ugly smile on his lips. "That's the worst? I'm still here, I still curse you."

On the television screen a young woman did a coarse Latin dance. She wore a low-cut dress and her breasts moved softly. At first Berman watched as though it were no more than a shadow on the ceiling. She turned her back and her buttocks moved swollenly. A sudden streak of desire ran through him and he observed it with the horror of someone watching a muscle spasm on an inert body, a thing with a semblance of having a separate life. Now weariness overcame him at the variety of armament his Enemy possessed. He got up with a moan and switched the set off. Then he threw himself on to the couch and watched the dot of light fade on the screen before a heavy, uneasy sleep took him. . . .

There was a warm, violet light. He could hear her slippered footsteps. Then she was standing over him with a sad, seductive smile on her mouth. Her hair was black as in the beginning but her face was covered with the familiarly loved lines. She nodded sweetly and bared her large white breasts to him. Lovingly he took their dark nipples in his mouth and felt, *felt,* the warm, moist weight of her. And he returned into her body so his heart sang. She was warm, enfolding. Then she was still and he felt the sudden piercing cold of her. Her body turned a chill, pallid brown, shriveled to a look of mummified age. . . .

"God almighty," he cried unknowingly, and woke sickened on his solitary couch, with the lust still despicably in him like a sullen rebel holding out against shame and bitterness, a spiteful thing which joined him in shaking his fist at heaven.

October, 1915

It had all been a nightmare to him, ever since the first stormy day out of Liverpool. And now, as he stood on the afterdeck in the suddenly glassy sea, it was still like living in a dream, though no longer a nightmare. His mother sat on the mound of her belongings, the feather bed, the copper pots, the dishes and linens and the small copper samovar. She lugged everything with her wherever she went, not trusting the hundreds of strangers they traveled with, and it was necessary for Berman to eat alone first so he could go out to guard her treasure while she ate.

They said the ship was only a day from America, and Berman watched the wheeling gulls, and wondered if they were American birds.

Except for the heavy swishing of the water under the ship as it lumbered swayingly through the lake-still ocean, there was no other sound but the harsh, pent-up moans of the laboring woman, hidden from his view by the backs of those who ministered to her. Someone had gone to find the ship's doctor in spite of everyone's insistence that it was not necessary.

"Who of us was brought into the world by a doctor?" a powerfully built woman with wide cheeks like a Chinese asked scornfully of all the immigrants. "And are we any the worse?"

But the woman who was a pharmacist's widow and used to

the finer things had gone anyhow, setting herself apart from all the rest.

So now it was a race against time for the midwives, a question of principle. They would bring this one out without the help of a man.

"Push, sweetheart, there's a darling . . . hard now, help him out to this funny world. . . . Work hard, come on, the harder you push the sooner you'll see his lovely face. . . . Press, press. . . ." The husky, Chinese-faced woman exhorted the straining woman on the coil of rope lovingly, gleefully, while all around the other passengers waited with varying expressions—some amused, some concerned, and some merely astonished, as though they, too, like Berman, fumbled in a dream.

Most of the people were drawn back from the immediate arena and the midwives made a little semicircle around the pale, sweating young woman on the pile of rope. Of all, Berman was the closest. He tried to keep his eyes averted from the glimpses of white leg he had between the broad backs of the attendants. For a while he pinned his gaze on his mother's figure, perched like a nesting bird on the great egg of her belongings. His mother nodded gently as she returned his look, and it was as though she answered a question in his eyes with that nod, as though she told him, "Yes, this is the way it was with me, too, this is the pain I suffered for you and it is right thus, you will bring this pain to a woman someday and that will be as it should be." And Berman thought in that moment that he had never seen anyone so strong and so wise as his mother, with her nodding face reddened by the setting sun, and he prayed to remember her that way no matter how old and ugly she might become.

Then there was a series of short, piercing screams from the laboring woman and the midwives cooed approvingly as they encouraged her to leap into the fray.

Unconsciously Berman moved closer and closer, so that soon

he was standing in full view of the proceedings. Stunned, he looked at the spread, bloody thighs with the small creature half-emerged from its mother's body, its eyes closed benignly as though totally unconcerned with all the drama surrounding it. The midwife's hands were stained with blood and there was a smell of it in spite of the gentle sea wind, so that Berman felt the blood was more potent than all of the ocean.

And then the baby was out, the cord severed and bound up, and the mother stilled by exhaustion. The Chinese-faced woman suddenly looked up from where she knelt with the baby dangling upside down from her powerful hands. Her face spread into a wild, furious smile. She slapped the tiny body several times until the baby's thin screech of indignation certified his existence. Then, with her eyes steady on Berman's stunned face, she passed the screaming, bloody baby up to him.

"Here, Big Eyes, here's a sample of the trouble you'll cause. . . . Go on, hold him, he's your brother and your son. How do you like it . . . a great thing, eh!" she cried with vicious affection.

And for a while Berman stood even deeper in the dream, with the ship rolling under him and the salty wind on his cheeks while the baby screamed up at him, beautiful and ugly in his mantle of blood, while all around the people laughed and called out joyful, teasing remarks and his own mother sat grinning at the wonder of it.

All day long Berman had a funny feeling about the cleaning woman in his house. Ruth had arranged with an employment agency for her to come and go over the house completely, and Berman had left the door open when he went with Riebold that morning. He didn't know what it was that bothered him, tried to explain it away by saying to himself, "There's nothing there for her to take. Anyhow, none of it means anything to me, bunch of junk." But really he knew his disturbance had nothing to do with any actual objects of value. It was almost as though he had some secrets there in those abandoned rooms, some guilt he felt might be exposed. Or perhaps there *was* something of a value he hadn't perceived, something a stranger could violate, something even he could violate.

It preyed on him to such an extent that even his work was affected. Heretofore nothing, not the worst heartache or worry, had ever been able to extend itself into that province which after all was by now almost exclusively a product of his body, an instinctive craft in which he was able to submerge himself, joylessly yet also without pain. But today things dropped from his hands, tools resisted him. He joined pipe joints sloppily and injured himself in countless small carelessnesses.

At one point he became enraged when Riebold tried discreetly to patch up the poor joint he had connected in the cellar they were working in.

"What do you think you're doing!" he snarled at the stooped figure of his partner. "Since when have you got any complaints how I do the work?"

"I'm not complaining," Riebold answered placatingly.

"Then what are you doing, going over something I already did? What am I, an apprentice? You're going to be forgetting who taught who this work pretty soon. Any time . . ."

"Don't carry on, Yussel, don't be ridiculous. You know me better than that. I know you, too, Yussel. I can tell when something is bothering you," Riebold said from the floor. "Your mind isn't on it, that's all right. How many times have you gone after me without saying a word? We never needed explanations, us two. Thirty years . . . listen, it's a long time. Don't get excited. You got something on your mind, okay, you don't have to talk about it. But the work? Fah, it's not important at our stage of the game. Forget it, huh? Go, go up to the truck, we'll knock off today."

And Berman went up the steps muttering, ashamed of his childish petulance, disturbed at the thought that phantom problems were able to cripple him now.

Riebold took him home in a discreet silence. Always the voluble one of the two, he had nevertheless always had an instinctive appreciation of his more taciturn partner's occasional strange moods. Possibly it was those peculiar depths in Berman, those periodic moments of seeming withdrawal from the immediate, which had made him love his friend with that blind and mystified love which is so much like reverence. It was as though he knew Berman saw much more than he did and therefore was able to suffer more complexly, more enduringly. "Ah, that Yussel," he was apt to say to his wife or to one of the men who knew Berman and complained of his occasional habit of looking through people in a manner that seemed rude and insulting. "Don't try to figure him, he's a dreamer, a miracle rabbi inside." He would speak proudly of it, knowing he didn't have the words for what he sensed in his partner, a mysticism or else a soul that could drink in many things and so was burdened beyond other people.

"Is there anything, Yussel?" he asked as the truck pulled up before Berman's house. "Something particular bothering you?"

Berman shrugged. "You know how it is with me—a million things."

"I know, I know. But today you really seemed specially upset. What is there today that got you so upset?"

"Ah, today, tomorrow, what's the difference," Berman said, glancing darkly toward the house. "Only Ruthie hired this cleaning woman to clean the rooms. . . ."

"So?" Riebold said, mystified.

"So I couldn't even tell you. Everything's strange lately. There's no explaining to somebody."

And Riebold nodded, respectful and compassionate for the dark complication of his friend's life.

"All right, Yussel, but you know, anytime you want me, I don't care when, the middle of the night . . ."

"Sure, sure, Leo, I know you," Berman said gently. Then he got out of the truck, waved briefly at his partner, and went up the steps as the truck roared slowly down the street.

First he smelled the alcohol, the sweet, nauseating pungence of it, exaggerated as though no breath of fresh air had come in to dilute it. Then, as though that were a sensory frame for her, he saw the woman, seated in his armchair with a cigarette in her hand.

"Oh, Mr. Berman, you must be Mr. Berman," she said, standing quickly, visibly startled by his sudden appearance. "I been goin' like a house on fire all day. Just thought I'd rest my legs a minute."

Berman nodded, expressionlessly, casting his eyes around at the room, which seemed as dusty and untouched as when he had left it that morning.

"I thought you'd be done," he said, not peevishly, not even disapprovingly, but rather as the statement of fact he intended. He felt the same unease he had felt all day, no more, no less, still unrecognizable. "It's enough, you can come and finish tomorrow."

"No, no," she insisted, walking rather too carefully past the vacuum cleaner, which stood in the dining room. "I just got a few little things to finish up. I'll go right ahead, don't you bother about me. Just do what you want, I won't be in your way."

She was a big, heavy-set woman with bleached hair and white, softly sagging skin that suggested she might once really have been blond. Her face still had the remnants of delicacy and Berman was reminded of certain Irish girls of his youth, those types of great, perishable prettiness he had dallied with before he was married.

"Just half a shake," she said from the sink, where she was filling a pail with hot water while the cigarette dangled from her mouth. "Just go over the kitchen floor a little. Won't take but a few minutes. I don't want to interrupt yer supper. Don't I know how it is with you hard-workin' men, hungry fer yer meal. Had it twenty-five years with my old man, like a bear when he came in. God help me if I didn't have somethin' hot waitin'. Carry on? My sweet Jesus, like a bear . . ."

"It's all right," Berman said. "No need to hurry. I can wait." Something strange and artificial sounded in his voice. He had the feeling he was acting out a part, falteringly, seriously, yet as though he were unsure of his lines.

"Oh, I know you men," she said, with a smile that revealed a great gap in her front teeth. "I oughta. Married twenty-five years. Old man set up big, sort of your build, strong. I bet

you're no weakling, no sir. . . . No, I know. . . ." She looked
at him teasingly from the corner of her eyes as she set the pail
down and lowered herself onto her knees. Then she set the
brush in the soapy water and leaned to her work, glancing up
at him now and then from her hands-and-knees position.

There was something overpoweringly bestial in her pose, an
attitude only magnified by those occasional upward glances
she cast. Her huge buttocks moved with her efforts and her
massive breasts swayed under her like those of a cow, restless
in the stall. And above the smell of soap and his own sweaty
body there was still the reek of alcohol that emanated from her.

"You found the whisky," he said, with a tiny bending of his
mouth which passed for a smile. The bottle stood unstoppered
by the kitchen sink, half-empty beside the octagonal glass she
had drunk from.

"I hope you don't mind, Mr. Berman. Just took a couple
little nips. I find it picks me up when I start feelin' low.
Medicinal, you might say. You oughta try it when you come
home all tired. Aw, big rough-type man like you, I bet you
done plenty drinkin' in your time," she grunted coquettishly.
"Don't I know you men. . . ."

And cued by the peculiar mystery of the role that possessed
him, Berman smiled, a great mouth-opened grin of alien mirth.

"I think I'll just take your advice," he said. He went to the
sink and poured the whisky into the glass smeared redly with
the woman's lipstick. "Medicinal," he said wryly, raising the
glass in a toast to her.

"Oh, now, you're pulling my leg," she said, instinctively
touching at the strawlike hair, which fell back over her face
right after.

Berman nodded, watching her over the glass with an odd
fixed glance as though through some unusual lens which dis-
torted his usual view.

"If you don't mind," she said, pushing herself up with a sigh and then standing with her back arched against her hand as though against a kink in her muscles, "I'd appreciate just a weeny little more of that stuff. Lord, I'm pooped, and *dry!*" She ran her tongue over thin lips artificially widened by lipstick.

Silently Berman handed her the glass and watched her take all that was left in it with her eyes assayingly on him all the while.

He seemed to be outside it, outside the tired, aging body in the dirty work clothes, watching with curious gaze the scene unfolding like a hazy movie in the austere kitchen.

When she emptied the glass and grinned at him, he went to the sink for the bottle. He got another glass down from the shelf, and then, with his back to her, still facing the cupboard and motionless as though gathering himself for some sudden and unwonted action, he spoke in a flat, one-toned voice.

"Sit down at the table." And then, faintly obligated to some nuance of human relationship, "Might as well relax. We both had a hard day."

For a moment there was silence. He could imagine surprise on her face, perhaps a shade of speculation. Then he heard the chair scrape out and her heavy sigh, which was an exclamation of relief and at the same time of resigned weariness for something she recognized that was as yet still beyond him.

"Your health," Berman said with a wide, grotesque smile that didn't involve his eyes. Together they threw their heads back in a swift gulp.

"Well-l-l-l . . ." She leaned comfortably forward against the table, pressing her great bosom into the edge so he could see the pillowing softness. "This is very nice of you, Mr. Berman. I tell you, most the people I come in contac' with ain't one quarter so considerate. Believe me, it's a pleasure to come in contac' with a human been once in a while. Oh-h-h-h, my achin' back. . . . Whew, just sittin' . . . and this beverage don't do no harm, not in the *least*." She smiled, close-mouthed against the missing teeth, and nodded her pleased acceptance of Berman's gesture toward the bottle. "This is nice. I tell you, if people would only sit and pass the time of day once in a while, believe me, there'd be a damn sight less trouble. Look, I'm widowed two years now and a girl gets mighty lonesome for just a friendly word sometimes. I bet you know what I mean, Mr. Berman. Now, the way I understand it, you're a widower yerself?"

Berman nodded as he stared into the glass at a drop that had eluded him.

"Well, then, you got some idea. It's no picnic, right? Oh, at my age—I'm forty-nine"—She watched him to see if her shaving of two years was noticed—"I don't need *romance*. Not that I'm not still a *real* woman . . ." She giggled archly. "But *companionship,* you know? I bet you get the same feelin'. Not, as I say, that a *real* man still wouldn't . . . Well-l-l . . . I'm just sayin'. . . . But *companionship* . . . that's the most important. . . ."

He kept nodding, no longer hearing her words as anything but a random clatter in the hard room. But his eyes took in with peculiar avidity the minutest details of her face and that part of her torso visible above the table: the red-veined, good-natured eyes; the white, sagging skin with its many blackish moles; the mouth, thin and corrugated; the ears, incongruously small and delicate, as if they were the one part of her not used since her youth. Her neck was thick, strong, and corded, and there was something oddly provoking in its beastlike strength, which ran down to her chest and the great pillows of her bosom.

"Oh, my goo'ness, I think I'm gettin' jus' a wee bit dizzy from this stuff. Proves I'm not one of these here habitual drinkers. Well, I'm with a gennelman—no danger . . . or is there?" She giggled and leaned back in her chair. "Well, this is sure swell, Mr. Berman. But I gotta think about the long trip home. Got to get my beauty rest. . . ."

She pushed herself to her feet and swayed uncertainly past his motionless figure.

And almost deliberately, as though under a compulsion not of his choosing, Berman rose and seized her from behind. He clasped at her mountainous breasts, began squeezing them in a pulsating rhythm which had none of the spontaneity of lust but only a sort of grimly dutiful viciousness.

"Oh-h-h-h, my goo'ness, Mr. Berman. Oh-h-h-h, you . . ." She leaned back against him, wearily yet almost happily, too, as though flattered by the recognition of her womanliness in spite of her own loss of interest in those things. "Yes, yes," she said comfortingly, covering his hands with her own over her breasts. You could tell she would go to great lengths for flattery. "You quiet ones . . . oh-h, my," she wheezed as she felt herself being propelled toward the bedroom, her clothes being unbuttoned all the while.

And once in the bedroom she disengaged his savage, pulling hands. "You can't figure out these things," she said in the bright light of the bedroom's overhead light as she grunted her arms behind her and unhooked her brassière.

Her naked body was enormous with flesh, quivering and nippled, thick with animal-like body hair.

"Come, sweetie, let me . . ." And she was against him, manipulating his body shamelessly, confident and experienced as though on old, familiar ground. "I know how it is with you men. Didn't I have it long enough? There, there, how's that?"

The lust grew out of him, was not intrinsic or part of his body, so it was a sickening thing. Mechanically he let his rough hands explore her sticky flesh, smelling sweat and alcohol and unidentifiable dirtiness.

Coquettishly she responded with some obscene tricks she had learned to perform expertly over the years.

And then there was a certain familiar depth of sensation begun in him and it was as though a wick had burned down to something terrifyingly powerful and explosive in him—a core that was packed with a sweet delicacy of memory. Like the antagonism of volatile chemicals, his body reacted in the ugly resemblance to something he had held beautiful. And there had never been such a maniacal rage in him as there was then. All that was mocking and grimly ironic in his fate smote him. His hate for a God with a human face became boundless.

"Aghhh, you!" he roared. Then he struck the spongy softness of her breast and there issued from him a sound between snarling and weeping.

He only struck her that once but she became breathless with shock at the sight of him. For a moment she was silent and then her throat shaped a small, wounded squeal. She hunched herself as though against invisible blows and stumbled over to her clothes. Berman reeled after her, mouthing words in Russian and Yiddish, words he didn't hear or understand himself, addressed to a torturer he couldn't see.

Then, somehow, she was dressed, or at least out of his sight with her clothes, and the words shrunk in his mouth. He never actually heard her go out. He just stood absolutely still for a long time in the hallway until, at some moment, he could tell he was alone in the house again.

For a little while he stood sniffing desolately in the long corridor, trying to clear his nose of the smell of sweat and alcohol. It seemed he would choke if he couldn't clear his nostrils, but then it occurred to him that wasn't why he was sniffing. Rather, he realized he was trying to find an elusive odor that no longer existed.

He began to beat his head gently against the invisible pattern of the hallway wall, thumping it in the rhythm of prayer, but senselessly, not aware of what he was doing, in the manner that ome babies put themselves to sleep. *Thump, thump, thump, hump,* went his head against the dark wall. It was the only ound in the world.

Berman stood with his head against the glass, looking out at the huddled houses, cold and inward-facing in the winter afternoon. This part of the village of Dolmyk was all Jewish and so it was quiet in the ebb of the Sabbath. With his forehead and eyes cold, his body warm in the heat of the fire, he couldn't have said whether or not he was happy. One part of him seemed obligated to chafe at the restriction his father placed on them all; he would have said to one of his friends that he wished for the outdoors. Yet there was a sweetness to his enforced brooding, a yearning he wouldn't have had if he could have gone about as he pleased. Instinctively he loved the order his father imposed, the shape and size the red-bearded man created with his laws. How would the wild moments in the field or by the river have value if there were no need to covet and hoard those minutes surrounded by his father's edicts? Not to say Berman actually asked himself that question; enough that he felt its truth in the wordless parts of his heart. And for now his mind was uncomplicated by words or real thoughts, but only abided in that tender daze, that state as distant from sadness as it was from joy. Comfortable, that's what he was; or safe, safe in a world of certainty.

He could almost predict when his father would take over the quiet sounds of the room with his deep, rumbling voice; he even had an idea what his father might say.

"All right, Rose, I will eat now."

There was the sound of his father's book slapping closed and the great, regretful sigh at the leaving of the Word. Then his mother made quicker sounds and began murmuring Berman's name, said it almost furtively as though not wishing to let her husband know that all things didn't magically await him.

"Sit, Yussele, sit," she hissed.

So Berman turned to the scene of the firelit table glowing with its white Sabbath cloth, glinting here and there with silver candlesticks that seized shards of fire in their polished surfaces. He encountered, too, the harsh, deep-eyed gaze of the man, disapproving with that part of his attention he allowed for small things, that consciousness he could spare from his communion with God.

His uncle and his cousin sat at the table hurriedly, throwing their coats over a chair as they went, hastening to cover their heads as the big man began intoning the *bruchah* over the bread.

Berman watched that massive face on which the flesh clung tightly to the mammoth bones and the red beard sprung like fire under its awesome architecture. His father prayed with his hands on his cheeks, and the hands, huge and dusty white from the flour he handled all week long, seemed like some crude carving in granite, animated in anger or fervor only by fantastic strength. Oh, Berman knew the weight of those hands, remembered the stunning disaster of being struck just once by them. When was the last time? Not since he was twelve, since that time he had fought with the carpenter's son in the weedy yard of the cheder and the teacher had led him home by the ear, there to offer him respectfully to the red-bearded man, going away with a little complacent smile, for he knew this was one father who did not shirk his duties.

They ate rich dumplings and black, soft meat surrounded by prunes and sweet potatoes and carrots in one savory thickness. His uncle Tobias held his mouth about three inches above the food and his hand was a blurring conveyor, so it seemed his plate emptied by magic; and his cousin Yankele ate with his usual blissful expression, eyes vacant over the bulging fact of his working jaws. There was a clinking and a clattering and the hoarse breathing of those heavy eating men, and all was warmth and nourishment within that room whose red sunset windows were translucent with frost, and the cold burn of the winter air reminded you of your good fortune, of God's grace in that heated room heavy with the cooked odors of meat and potato and groats.

And since everything was as it should be, the atmosphere lightened with the darkness drawn over the Sabbath. Berman's father sat back on pillows and talked with his brother Tobias, or rather let the smaller man talk, only interjecting words from time to time in his heavy voice, whose ponderousness caused you to imagine great significance in each little phrase. His mother sighed contentedly as she gathered the dishes for the ritual of washing, for in that house everything was a ritual . . . like the slanting of the breadboard by Yankele as automatically the two boys began the game with the walnuts.

They rolled the uneven spheres of the nuts down the incline, gave little giggles when one nut hit another. Berman cracked one and began eating the sweet, woody meat, and Yankele reproached him, saying, "The game, come on, the game."

So it was nothing untoward, either, when the red-bearded father stood up in his towering strength and stretched noisily as he said to the gathering, "I'll rest awhile. You'll call me soon, Rosele, for tea." And he strode unhurriedly to the bedroom, which showed only as a doorway of darkness from where the boys squatted on the floor.

But a few minutes later the calm, sonorous voice came out of the bedroom and the house was riven.

"Rosele, Yussel, Tobias, Yankele," the father called.

A trembling began deep inside Berman, began to spread to his chest and legs and arms; he seemed seized with a spasm of cold. He followed his mother, who ran with her hands over her mouth. Behind him his uncle and his cousin moaned in fear, and Tobias uttered monotonous oaths at the terror of the un- known.

Berman's mother lit the lamp. There was his father, as huge and powerful as ever, except for a tiny, dark trickle of blood, dull beside the magnificence of the beard as it ran down from the corner of his mouth and lost itself in that brighter red.

"Raise the pillow behind me, Rosele. Don't talk. I have no time. I am dying. I would kiss you all and give you my bless- ing. . . . Silence, woman, there will be time for tears . . . not for me. . . . Ah-h-h-h, I will pray for you, Rosele, from Heaven. Tobias . . . Yankele . . . Yes, yes, so it is sudden. Life is sudden. . . . Death . . . You are alive until the moment of death. . . . What is the surprise on your faces? I am not surprised. . . . My Kaddish, where is my Kaddish?" he grunted, searching through his darkening vision for Berman. "Ah, there . . . Kiss your father, I will live with God. . . . And your brother . . . where? America . . . some dark place . . . He, too, the Kaddish . . . I will know. . . ." Only then did the face lose its power. The mouth opened in the midst of flaming hair, the eyes dulled and went out, the color faded to bloodlessness under the skin. And soon the face was no more than a monument, a noble structure housing nothing.

Berman's mother began the terrible wailing, and it seemed to Berman that he had known the sound of that grief all his life or known that it existed, for he seemed to recognize it as something preordained. And even the awful knot in his own chest and his painful crying were something he had expected unconsciously, something he had built himself for.

The grieving woman tore at her hair, came out with black handfuls from the head she had freed of the marriage wig. And her screaming became louder from the physical pain as the roots of her scalp were ripped out, so she fell into a fervor, a rhythm they all began rocking to, Berman and his cousin and his uncle, finding a bleak comfort in that, an outlet for pain and shock.

The women came in from the dark streets, huddled under their shawls, commiserating, ready to cry with the new widow, yet businesslike and calmly efficient for all their consoling wails and tears. With practiced hands they carried the corpse into the living room and removed the clothes. Huddled, shapeless in their thick shawls and *babushkas,* they washed the great white body with its outrageous patches of red hair resembling life. They splashed in the basin and slapping sounds came from the cloths they ran lovingly over the still shape. The candles they had placed at the four corners of the body cast a confusion of darkness, double shadows of their ministering figures on the length of white flesh.

Berman stood as though paralyzed, his eyes straining in their sockets. It was as though the terrible scene were too huge for him to take in. He held his mouth open, too, spread his hands. Dumbly he practiced the words of the Kaddish, the prayer for the dead. It had no relevance to what he saw and felt in his heart.

The next day the air was filled with snow, the road and fields swollen with the white masses of it. Berman trudged through its depths, following the wagon which swayed from side to side, trying to follow in the ruts left by the wheels. Bits of snow fell from the wheels as they reached the top of their revolution. His nose was filled with the stinging sharpness of the tiny crystals which blew off the coffin. But his eyes were blind, reddened by the scene of the previous night, and the snow was blotched with the color of blood for him.

And yet, and yet, strangely, his grief came out in a shape like beauty. He was filled with wonder, brimming with the peculiar beauty he felt like an inexplicable pain.

Going up his front steps he almost had the feeling of being physically engaged in some worn piece of machinery. There was a sense of automation, of knowing exactly what each movement would be, one after another, like a movie he had sat through innumerable times. There was no pleasure in it, only a sort of bleak ease, for it demanded nothing from him.

Push upward slightly as you turn the key. Door squeaks at the point of half-opening. Electric bill falls from the letter slot. And the *Jewish Ledger*. Walk through the living room and the dining room, careful to walk on the runner instead of the carpet. Through the kitchen where the stove rattles to your footfall, loud after the muffling carpets in the front rooms. Down the long hallway, past the bedrooms where nothing stirs, not even the curtains, for the windows are closed tight as though sealed. Into the bathroom where all the mirrors show a strange old man who glances stonily once at you through his dirtied glasses and then pays no more attention. Turn on the water, three-quarters hot, one-quarter cold, so it comes out mixed just right through the single modern faucet. But it whines, something needs tightening, a new washer, needed it for years; like she used to say, "The plumber's house always has leaky faucets." Like she used to say . . . Then strip the greasy clothes

128

and stand in undershorts before the basin of water. Slosh the warm water over the white, sagging flesh, the ugly lumps of dried, hard muscle, almost obscene without firm flesh to grace it. Then dry with the worn, thin towels that get sopping wet so quickly. Couldn't throw things away, that woman. Why? Because it was hers, because everything that was hers was precious to her: husband, daughters, son, towels, everything. Then pad back into the kitchen, bare feet slapping on the cool linoleum, feeling clean, dry, like a washed pebble. Take down the small, polished frying pan, gleaming from thousands of loving sessions with the steel wool. Take two eggs from the refrigerator, with the cold air on your body, your glasses fogged so the kitchen is a dreamlike place for a moment. Then no longer a dream. Set the butter to sizzling, crack the eggs and drop them hissing on the yellow bubbling. The clearness dims, turns opaque, white, the edges brown a little. Slip the spatula under the eggs, awkward with its handle missing—nothing thrown out. The water hot in the kettle, pour it over the Swee-touch-nee bag in the thick glass. Sit, break off a piece of challah, pour salt, from the ornate little silver tower, a wedding gift, bereft of its lost mate, the pepper shaker, lost in a summer move to the cottage, twenty, twenty-two, years and years ago. Then eat, slowly, neatly ("He never even needs a napkin, my Joe," she used to say), eyes toward the window, seeing nothing, only light and shape, wavering shadows cast by the lowering sun through a tree. . . . A tree? What tree? I never noticed a tree there. . . . What kind . . . elm, maple, oak? A patch on the screen, double mesh, rusting, should have been aluminum, ah, well. A sound of a lawn mower. There he goes again with his gardening, that idiot. Stand by the window, sipping the tea from the glass through the cube of sugar in the mouth so the liquid is turned sweet at the portal. Watch him, that jerk in his natty Bermuda shorts, his yellow sport shirt, his straw gardening cap, wearing new work gloves out of which come the soft, muscleless arms.

Pushing the little mower over the short, tender grass. His *exercise!* What, is he stopping already, tired from that little work! Oh, the woman, his wife, she's bringing him lemonade, smiling at him. . . . Aghhh, fools, stupid fools. Wash the dishes in the twilight. Slosh, slosh, what an ugly sound. Then turn the light on, go to the drawer where the bridge pads, the pencils are. Take out the cards, thickened and dark at the edges from wear. Then sit down at the kitchen table. Shuffle them. The riffling sound, a pleasant sound. Shuffle again and again for the sound, staring past the cards at the patterned oilcloth, an old pattern. Lay them out, the friendly faces of the jacks. Ah, an ace, two, three. Now, which pile to put the nine on. Dark outside, humming. Enough with the cards. Put them back in the drawer with the bridge pads and the pencils. Go over the wooly carpets to the living room. Turn the television on. Ah-h-h-h. Warmth seems to emanate from the lighted screen. His mouth relents from the hard line, opens a little. Sett e back in the chair. A row of wooden, false-fronted buildings, a Western town. There he is on the *faird,* the horse. Tough looking, don't worry about him . . . Eyes heavying, mouth stretching in yawns. Shut off the television, watching regretfully how the picture shrinks in toward the middle to a little bright square, a dot, extinction. Go back into the kitchen. Put the light under the kettle again after shaking it to make sure there's enough water. A fresh Swee-touchnee tea bag. Moving with the drowse on you so it is like a ritual. But it is not. Stately as though in a dream. But it is no dream, no dream. . . . And then into the bedroom and on to the bed of nails with a bland, dead face.

July, 1912

They were too old for that kind of play; Berman knew it and so did the other boys. Yet here they were again, throwing potatoes at each other in the dusty field, out in the broad evening sunlight, while everything around them—the woods and all the country beyond the village—had now entered into the transitory shadows. The trick was to snap your wrist as you swung the long, pointed stick. Like that . . . uh . . . so the small brown potato flew off like a bullet. They were too old for it so it assumed a greater pleasure, as if now it was an outlet for their new, subtle desires, a symbol of things they yearned for with their inarticulate cries. There was a wildness to the potato battles now, a gay menace in the viciousness of their throws. They tried to hurt each other and even their cries of pain had a savage ecstasy. It was *feeling* they were after, a sense of heart and body bound together. Pain, causing pain—both or either, they were confused—seemed the same.

Swish went Berman's stick. *Zi-i-i-i-p* went the tiny brown shape through the golden air, an extension of his arm, as though his arm could reach infinite distances. *Whap!* His cousin Yankel clapped his hand to his forehead.

"Yee-e-e-e," one of the boys shouted, moving crouched over in a threatening circle. There were no sides, no teams. Each of them was against all the others. Or with them in that unknown joy. Their shadows were long over the lumpy, dusty ground, the shadows increasing them, covering areas far larger than their own bodies.

Berman laughed loudly, a braying sound full of excitement and menace and pity; laughed at the brown smudge on his cousin Yankel's long, gentle face; laughed at the boy Avrom, who wore a lion's stalking expression on his long-lipped rabbit face. And laughed, too, with his cry of pain as the hard, unripe potato clubbed his temple so that his whole body twitched with shock.

Then he, too, crouched in elaborate caution, his stick held back, the potatoes in his shirt rolling forward. Clods of dried earth crunched under his feet. He measured the distance to Avrom, tensed his arm to throw. . . .

Then he felt the hard blow against the back of his head with a force that showed it came from very close. So he whirled with his head ringing and threw himself on the gangly figure of his cousin Yankel and rolled with him on the ground, his mouth opened in laughter so the dust rolled in and made grittiness against his teeth. He was crushed, then, by the heavy body of Avrom, and they rolled all three on the dusty ground with the hard lumps of the potatoes fallen from their shirts digging into them, moving them so it seemed the earth joined in their violent play. Screaming their inchoate calls under the clear evening sky. And Berman, pinned for a moment with his eyes up to the rosy blue, saw crows dipping like slow-falling, black darts, and rising again on their shadowy wings. Elbows struck his face, someone's head drove a tingling pain into his nose, and he tasted salt and jammed home pain to his cousin's face gratefully, yelling the wild laughter under the Russian sky. Struggling, feeling his bruised body, grappling frantically for limbs forever out of reach, for a victory just a hair out of grasp. Dizzy and breathless, choking in the dust that lay only close to the ground where they writhed, while up above the air was clear and cool.

And finally, when the wrestling lost its savor, was exposed as merely the substitute for the unnamable yearning, they lay back panting, tired and suddenly dull. It was as though what they had thought to seize turned out only a breath, a scent, a thing as yet remote from them. The sky darkened, turned bluer, like water, showing greater and greater depths. The mocking call of a small bird came up from the tall grasses at the edge of the potato field and a lone crow carried the message in his coarser voice into the wood. Up close there was only the sound of their panting breaths, so loud in its volume that all the other sounds of nature were as silence beside it.

Until the girl's laughter startled them and sat them up and they stared stupidly at the figure tall from the ground.

"If you could see yourselves, what a sight," she said, a slender girl with sallow, unhealthy-looking skin and black, feverish eyes. "Do you pick potatoes with your teeth? Or perhaps you think you are worms grubbing for the little green bugs?" She began to laugh, pointing her finger at them each in turn, Avrom, Yankel, and Berman.

"Go on," Avrom growled, getting to his feet and swiping vigorously at his dirty clothes. "Get the hell away from here, Rachel!" They knew her well as a wildly silly girl given to hysterical shrieking and hectic laughter. Like a familiar thorn they removed her with shouts and insults whenever she intruded on their games.

But now, strangely, they felt themselves under a peculiar constraint. Berman looked at the coarse brown cotton of her dress and it seemed to him she had brought something different and disturbing with her.

"What are you doing here?" he asked her.

And the quietness of Berman's voice cast the other boys into a profound unease, for they all felt a connection now between the mad scrambling on the ground and this strained, unusual response to the girl.

"The same thing you are," she said, her mouth curved in a secret smile, her eyes on Berman only, as though her choice was so quixotic and random that his speaking first made him her choice.

"Why aren't you playing the silly games with the other girls?" Berman asked, standing up with all the dirt on him, his hands immobile at his sides as though a weird flash of pride prevented him from brushing himself off before her.

"Because I prefer boys," she answered levelly, her thin mouth still smiling.

"She's a little touched," Yankel jeered, uncertainly. "Go on, madwoman, get back to your crazy . . ." The quiet and the peculiar reserve of the other boys made his voice dwindle.

"And which boys in particular?" Berman asked, rising to an odd bravery, for he felt a sudden desperation that mystery might elude him forever if he didn't explore its every offer. "Or perhaps one boy . . ."

She studied him then, her smile suddenly wiped off in an access of puzzlement or maybe even fear.

"Perhaps one boy," she agreed.

And Yankel and Avrom got up silently, as much awed by their own instinct of discretion as they were by the strange sense of a compact being made. Oh, they knew by then all the simple aspects of sex and procreation. What boys of fifteen in a small village surrounded by farms and the abundance of fertility didn't! They had hooted and shared the rich, sly humor of the peasants as they watched the stud horses fulfill their bought and paid-for lust, had crouched unobtrusively in the meadows in spring observing the rams go about their wall-eyed orgies with the phlegmatic ewes, and had drawn nasty delight in resemblances to people of the village. But certain things were beyond them, and among the mysteries was the aspect of solitude in love-making among humans, the only-guessed-at attitude of that strange and familiar animal called woman. They were, all three, brought up to the rules of sanction and ritual, and usually thought there were many years between them and possible initiation. Yet here they were, in the dusk of the potato field, suddenly encountering what they could feel to be a sacrosant entrance, sensing it without the evidence of experience but only in that most powerful of indicators, their senses. So with a solemnity and seriousness that was new and embarrassing to them, they exchanged flat glances with each other, gave a brief, charged gaze at the back of Berman's narrow head and beyond it to the onyx-eyed girl with her head cocked in a bemused contemplation that rendered her quite unlike the girl of familiar and revolting craziness, and then walked off, wordless and full of unaccustomed dignity, which prevented them from running or even brushing at their clothes. It was as though they had stepped unobtrusively into the adult world of appearances and something had come between them, unavoidable, unforgivable.

Now Berman felt his heart beating uncomfortably in his throat as he stood alone with the girl. In a sort of panic he tried for the nonsense of their old relationship.

"So, Goat Girl, what were you bleating about? Must you bother us always? Go, go to your crazy games."

"Do you want me to go?" she asked.

Berman shrugged.

"Come, go, as you want."

"Perhaps I'll go, then," she said.

And Berman looked up at her, too proud to tell her not to, yet afflicted enough with hunger so that it showed in his eyes.

"Or maybe I'll take a walk. . . . Will you come with me, Yussel?" she asked, already starting away in the direction of the woods.

Without answering he began to walk, at first a little behind her, then, fully committing himself, alongside. He had the feeling that eyes watched from behind them, from the direction of the village. Once he whirled around to see but there were only the lights of the houses through the trees and the smoke from some late supper fires curling up against the sunset.

They walked some distance, through a dense part of woods, then out to a little clearing where there were the remains of an ancient peasant hut. Buttercups grew over the humble ruins and there were fireflies on the ground darkness. The sky overhead was violet, and back to the east there were hazy summer stars in the part of the heavens already claimed by night.

Rachel sat down with her back to a silvery beech tree and Berman joined her, sitting silently, clasping his knees and gazing out at the glade in an attitude of intense preoccupation.

"Do you think I'm pretty, Yussel?" she asked in a soft, murmurous tone.

Berman raised his shoulders in a mild shrug, his eyes still intent on the twilight.

"Why did you come with me?"

"I don't know," he said.

"Because you like me? Something about me . . ."

He squinted now as though trying to pierce that illusory light.

"Answer me!"

"I don't know why I came with you. That's the truth," he replied, still looking away from her, sitting almost motionless as though he imagined himself to be on the edge of a fall he wasn't sure he wished to precipitate. "Some reason why . . . And you?" he said, turning toward her at last, impatient now with his hesitancy after the time and effort he had expended in this peculiar vagary. Her face was a luminous oval in the half-light, the unhealthy complexion and frantic eyes benefited by the unrealistic dusk.

"I like you . . . best of all the boys. . . . I would have gone with you before but you mocked me. Now, tonight, I felt it was different, that you would want to go with me. . . . And you did . . . you wanted to."

Berman nodded slowly, an expression of gravity on his face as though he wished to impart great logic to her faltering answer.

"Yes, that's true, I did, I wanted to."

She was silent for a moment. Then she spoke firmly as though as a result of her careful consideration.

"Shall we kiss each other, then?"

Berman nodded, unable to speak.

"Well . . ."

He sighed as he turned toward her, a sound of great resignation. There were many things in his mind to overcome in those seconds as he moved on his knees toward where she sat unmoving against the tree.

There was a moment of groping, trying to find her mouth. Her face was a blur up close. And then it was surprisingly warm. . . . A mouth . . . how strange . . . half-opened to his . . . a mouth, an ordinary mouth. He felt a warm excitement impossible to localize at first, leaned more heavily on her. And then he began to recognize some of the aspects of their closeness, like a traveler coming upon landmarks someone has told him to look for. Her thin arms went around his neck. He squeezed her tightly and she made an awkward little sound.

"Kiss me, kiss me," she cried softly.

"That's what I'm doing," he moaned.

"Oh, you," she breathed, exasperated and passionate.

His hand went up to fondle the tiny protuberance of her breast. She began kissing him all over his face, making little sucking sounds like some sort of insect.

Then the wildness he had felt in the potato field returned to him and he lost sight of everything but that will to feel, to inflict. He rubbed her bare legs and up to the delicate heat of her groin. Madly he sought to experience more than was possible, would have gone through her, consumed her. He forgot who she was, indeed who he was himself. They tossed on the ground in an agony of bewilderment and painful joy. He heard her crying and distantly pitied her even as he would have annihilated her. Except that suddenly he was gushing his lust all by himself, moaning as at a terrible loss.

He rolled away from her and lay with his head in his hands, feeling soiled and frightened and immeasurably changed.

"Oh, Yussel," she said, her crying stopped now that the danger was over. "What we did . . . Do you love me?"

"Yes, yes, all right . . ."

And they sat for some time in the dark wood, driven to alien silence, staring at the buttercups sprinkled over the formless ruins, vivid and white in the moonlight like snow.

When he entered his house that night, his father looked up from his book and Berman stood still, enduring the dark, penetrating study. For a moment anger filled his father's eyes, then a glint of something Berman imagined to be sadness. Finally he turned back to his book and waved his son away.

"Go to bed and God keep you," he said.

The next day he saw her with a group of girls. She was laughing more loudly than all the rest, screaming in her frantic, hectic amusement. For an instant her eyes met his and she was still, her mouth opened on some deadly wound. But only for a second or two, so no one could tell except him. Then she was on her way, looming taller than the others, noisy and foolish as always.

She looked uglier than he had remembered her, yet somehow powerfully touching, like something lost which had been of great value.

"Crazy Rachel," said Yankel, glancing sideways at Berman, then questioningly at Avrom.

"Crazy Rachel," Berman agreed.

Then he punched his cousin and ran off tauntingly. He laughed as though he hadn't a sadness in the world.

CHAPTER THIRTEEN

He had supper at Riebold's house and afterward, in the tor-turous cheer of Ethel Riebold's chatter as she cleared the dishes, they had three or four shots of whisky while they played two-handed pinochle for pennies.

Riebold reminisced gently, carefully, checking his friend's face as he brought up the more distant memories, those that had as little to do with Mary Berman as possible. He was try-ing his own brand of therapy on his partner, unobtrusively, with a discretion no one would have believed of that apparently simple man. Really he worked at it every hour of the day he spent with Berman, so mildly and carefully that he thought Berman as yet had not been aware of it. Evenings with his wife he planned the next day's little gestures and conversations with great deliberation and with a patience that astounded himself, never going beyond the cautious confines he had set for him-self. "What you do for that man," Ethel Riebold had said more than once, not with any disapproval but rather in amazement, perhaps a little wistfully, as though wondering if the coarse, good-natured man would have expended as much of himself on his own wife. Riebold's response was always the same, a little impatient and chiding. "He would do much more for me if it came to that! Besides, he's very important to me." And then, as though embarrassed at the sentimental sound of that, he would amend, "Do you think I could run this business by myself? I would lose my shirt."

"Yussel," Riebold said, chuckling as he pondered the cards so as not to make the reminiscence too important. "Do you know what I was thinking of today, for no special reason—just like that?"

Berman shook his head as he rearranged his hand. The whisky on top of the unaccustomed quantity of good, home-cooked food had him feeling a numbness he could mistake for relaxation.

"I was remembering that time—oh, it was a good fifteen, sixteen years ago—when we took that long auto trip. You remember, the six of us—you and Mary, Ethel and me, and Fox and his wife. That time, where was it, in New Hampshire or someplace, when we waited too long to find a place to stay and we ended up, the six of us sharing the one room. How silly we were, laughing and all. And then, after we quieted down . . . You remember there was a pot in the room we had joked we could use if anyone had a emergency. And all of a sudden, when it got quiet, there was the sound of like someone pissin' in the pot, and Mary yelled out loud because it was right by her bed. So we turned on the light and there was Fox pouring a glass of water into the pot right beside your bed and how we laughed. . . ."

"Enough, enough," Berman growled. "We were playing cards. What are you hocking my head with all that!"

And Riebold's face whitened a little with hurt as he looked, abashed, at his wife. She only turned her head away, forbearing, avoiding the I-told-you-so look that tempted her, only pitying her husband with his strange, difficult love for this stranger who used to be their dearest friend.

So they played a while longer, in a strained silence broken only by the sound of the cards and the woman's work with the dishes. Finally, Berman pushed the cards away and stood up, his hands spread appealingly.

"Look, Ethel, Leo, I'm not good company, this is no good. . . ."

"Oh, don't be silly, Joe," they protested.

"Wait, wait," he said, holding up his hands against their kindness. "It's true, no sense pretending not. I'm out of it but I still got eyes, that much I can see. I make you uncomfortable and I don't do me any good, either. Like before, with that story . . . Listen, Leo, I know you inside out. You been trying all along to bring me out of it. . . . You done good, too, not too obvious, clever, I was amazed. But I knew all along. And the truth is I was so grateful for what you were trying that I could have cried sometimes. It's no use though, Leo. . . . There's nothing anyone can do for me. I'm not going into it, there's no words. Only I can tell you this: Mary's death isn't all of it;— that was just the last straw, the worst. . . . What He's done to me . . . what a joke He's played on me all along . . ." His voice shook with rage, his lips whitened.

Riebold half-stood, Ethel reached out her hand from the other side of the room; their faces were grave and pitying.

Berman took a deep, quieting breath, exhaled it slowly.

"Don't try to figure. . . . It's my battle. Your pretty little memories, jokes . . . I have no sense of humor any more. Better you should leave me alone. Live your nice, sweet lives, please. Don't let me start telling you what I think of it. . . . Go, count me out. I love you, but leave me out of it."

He walked away from the kitchen, leaving them in similar poses of dreamy regret, their heads bowed so that it seemed they were ashamed without knowing why. Then he went out their front door into the summer evening, murmurous with the countless sounds of insects and human beings, of hoses hissing softly and gliders creaking on rusty chains, and he felt oddly comfortable and isolated from all those sounds. He attributed his peculiar ease to the effects of the whisky, and thinking of that he wondered why he hadn't thought to buoy himself before with whisky. He thought of the night he had drunk with the woman.

Then he noticed a small boy walking alongside him, peering up at his face curiously. It occurred to him that he had been registering his thoughts on his face. He smiled thinly at the child, who was barefooted and skinny.

"I make funny faces, don't I, sonny?" he said.

The boy stuck his tongue out at him and dashed to a porch. A woman was standing there, looking a little apprehensively at him.

Berman shrugged.

"Nice boy." he said.

She smiled politely and drew the child close to her.

Berman saw how he looked to her and understood her trepidation. A bulky, shambling old man with a cold face that could not be warmed by a polite smile, a homely old man, neat and clean now in a sport shirt and pressed slacks. But alone, walking all alone in the summer night, in no hurry to get any place, and so suspect, cryptic, unknowable like a shade, fearsome in his quiet, unhurried attitude, behind the glasses that obscured his eyes, or showed something different there at every different reflection.

The house was hot after the cooled air of the evening. Berman began opening all the windows, bringing the tiny, ringing sounds of the crickets into the rooms, the hum of distant car motors and the far-off baying of a dog.

He was in his daughters' room when the phone rang. It startled him and he lost his sense of direction for a moment in the unlit room. He cracked his shin against the corner of the bed in his hurry and gasped until he reached the phone.

"It's me, Daddy," his daughter said gently, reassuringly, as though she thought she had awakened him with her call.

"Yes," he said, pulling a kitchen chair under him and sitting to face the window, which looked almost as bright as daylight in contrast to the dark room.

"I haven't spoken to you in two days. Why don't you call me sometimes?"

"Well, you know, I don't think of things. I have enough trouble to remember to pay the electric bills. . . . None of these things did I ever do. . . ." He still felt faintly the torpor from the whisky, thought he would like to have another drink before it wore off. "I think about you, the children. I just don't think about calling."

"Daddy . . ."

"Yes?"

"Daddy, don't you want me to be—relieved? Oh, I know you're tired of hearing it. But for me, for *me* . . ."

"Please, Ruthie, no more now. When the time comes that I want to come live there I'll tell you. Believe me, I won't be shy. Not yet . . ."

"I just don't see the sense in it. You're not the only one in mourning, you know." She seemed to be crying a little. "Why can't we be sad together, comfort one another? Do you have any idea how you break my heart, how I feel, thinking of you all alone there, like a hermit?"

"You got no idea, you're just a child," he said a little angrily. "I'm not in the same boat with you. Let me tell you something. You talk about sad, about mourning. That's what you got. It's different. What you got is like a sad movie. You think about the old times, about the things that are over and done with anyhow, and you're sad, you cry a little, for the good old days." His voice was raspy, harsh, and scornful in the mouthpiece, and no sound came from the receiver except the faint sibilance of his daughter's breathing. "Listen to me, Ruthie, it's not that way with me at all! Tonight I was by Riebold for supper and he started bringing up something that happened years ago. So careful he is, afraid to say the wrong thing, I might get hurt. You know all I felt? I'll tell you—*irritated!* See, I'm not crying for the good old days. I'm crying because I'm dead . . . worse than dead . . . in Hell. I feel only hate. Oh, how could I tell you? I can't go to you like I am. I would poison your whole house." He was silent for a moment; when he spoke again it was in a cold, almost cruel voice. "I can't help you *mourn,* I can't be *sad* with you. I'm a million miles underneath sad."

There was only the sound of her crying in the receiver when he hung up. He sat back in the chair for a few minutes to re-trieve the silence. Then he got up and went to the cabinet for the bottle of whisky and filled a water glass two-thirds full. He gulped about half of it down, then took the bottle and the glass with the remaining whisky to the table and sat down. Carefully he arranged bottle and glass so they made two points of a triangle completed by himself. He took several more sips from the glass. When he put it down he wasn't satisfied with its relationship to the bottle and to himself, moved it an inch, moved it back, then moved the bottle. His hands were light blurs in the dark room, seemed disembodied, ending at the wrists, which in spite of their thick muscularity looked delicate and vulnerable. He sat there fussing with the bottle, occasionally drinking, refilling the glass, moving the two objects. Outside, the night was alive with little sounds: tinklings, chirpings, buz-zings. Inside there was just the inhuman sound of his swallow-ing and the little bumps of the glass and the bottle as he moved them in undecipherable patterns.

He guessed he was drunk. His hands seemed an impossible distance from his invisible self. Most of the taste of the whisky was lost on him by now but a faint, nauseating essence came through to him and made him feel a little sick to his stomach.

"Oh, well," he said as he stood, offhand, as though at some tiny consideration like the putting out of a light.

Slowly he walked down the hall to the bathroom. The light there was a sudden violence and he squinted his eyes. He opened the medicine cabinet, swinging the sight of his face away with the opening of that mirrored door. There were two or three razor blades on the bottom shelf. He studied them for a moment, then selected the one that had no visible rust on it. He closed the cabinet door but kept his head down so the face couldn't look at him.

Absently he ran the blade across the inside of his wrist in two deliberate strokes. Then he put the blade down on the sink and watched the two fine lines redden and thicken with blood, which hung in the markings for a considerable time, held by the surface tension, until finally, like a river overrunning its banks, it began to flood his wrist with a dozen little meandering streams. He held his arm out from his clothes as he moved over toward the toilet. Then he held it over the bowl, watching how the thick drops fell into the water in the toilet and spread there like veinous red blossoms.

Some of the blood began to run up his arm, so he tilted his hand lower. His wrist was a wild crimson smear. Curiously he studied it, tried to find importance in that innocuous, gaudy color.

Then he noticed the red splashings on the floor, one spot on the immaculate gray throw rug. He made a little clucking sound behind his teeth. Aimlessly he moved back to the sink, began washing his wrist. The water ran pink in the bowl and he was amused at how tiny the cuts were with the flow rinsed away. Unhurriedly he dried his arm off with toilet paper. Then he opened the cabinet and took out the gauze and the tape. It was hard binding the wrist up. He had to use his teeth to tighten the knot. Hardly any of the blood came through the bandage and he guessed it would stop bleeding soon with the pressure of the dressing.

He cleaned out the sink, flushed the toilet, and put the razor blade, the gauze, and the tape away. It all had such a deliberate feeling that it seemed to Berman less an act and a changed decision than some particular, planned ceremony.

His head felt light and useless. Almost childishly, he put his head all the way back and stared upward, not seeing the ceiling or anything else. He began to chuckle without his mouth changing expression, his face impassive and unsmiling, looking as though something separate inside him made that sound and he had no part in it.

September, 1910

From inside the synagogue he could see the autumn sunshine only as a dusty light on the dirty windows. All around him was the murmurous sound of the men praying, their shoulders white with prayer shawls like the peculiar uniforms of a slumbering army. There was a strong smell of bad breath from his father on one side of him and his brother on the other. It was always that way by the afternoon of the Fast. No water had passed their mouths since the afternoon before and the sourness increased with the passing hours. And it was dim, close with the re-used air of a hundred bodies, while outside there was that fresh, sunlit air.

His eyes swam over the Hebrew letters in his prayer book and his head ached with weakness. Yet there was an odd pleasure in his weakness, too, a feeling like the dreaminess of fever. He no longer was bored as he had been in the morning when his body had still been fresh and strong from sleep and the nourishment of the previous night's supper. The restlessness was quenched in the strange susceptibility of his senses. The big, musty room took on an exotic quality, an air of foreignness. He seemed transported to some place of great distance, of great height. His father loomed immense and godly, eyes closed under the jutting shelves of his brows as though before some intense light which Berman could not see. His red beard was the brightest thing there and all the roomful of people seemed to revolve around that mass of color, all their voices become mere accompaniment to the low, brooding voice that came from it. The Lion of Judah shone in its gilt paint over the Ark and there was something so enigmatic in the velvet-covered Torah that he could imagine a gigantic form compressed in its twin cylinders.

Above, on the railed balcony where the women sat, his mother rocked in the rhythm of the prayers.

Occasionally a little swirl of fervor would trail through the drone as one man after another raised his voice. It sounded as though they discovered little nuggets of superb beauty in the pages, and Berman looked at the black shapes of the words to find the treasures. They were beyond him, and he returned to his own feverish treasure, which was unnamable and all around him.

Some of the windows were still covered with boards from the destruction of the year before. He remembered the terror and the awe, the wonder of his father then.

Gradually a ringing filled his ears. The white prayer shawls blurred before his eyes. He fixed his eyes on his father's huge, white-dusted hands, on which the red hairs shone exaggeratedly. The hands grew in his vision, the ringing increased to fill the room and he lost the sound of the monotonous praying. Someone would hear it, he worried, fearful of his father's anger. His body tilted . . . or the room. Darkness filled his view. He fainted.

When he opened his eyes he saw the sky and the faces of his mother and father. The fresh pungence of the air intoxicated him but he felt completely strengthless and lay without moving.

"It is all right for him to have some food," his mother said angrily. "He is still a child. Must he get sick, die?"

"Hush, woman! It is Yom Kippur, a day of atonement.

Stop your prattling about sickness and death." He looked down at his son and Berman saw the brilliant blue of the man's eyes, so that as he looked up at him like that, with the sky beyond, it was as though his father's eyes were holes through which Berman could see the sky. "He will not eat until the sunset," he said in a stern voice. "Do you understand, my son?"

"I would not break the Fast, Father," Berman said in a weak voice from the ground.

"No, you would not," the man said gently.

Then the great face softened and a smile appeared for just a moment on the crude, harsh mouth.

Berman could not remember ever having seen his father smile. He gazed up at that brief transfiguration and his eyes suddenly swam with tears as at the sight of something so rare and lovely that he knew grief even at the moment of his joy, for he knew it would be lost to him forever.

And then his father's face was gone and he lay for some time on the ground, staring up at the sky. Finally he felt a little stronger and his mother allowed him to sit up against the trunk of a tree. They sat, the two of them, in the sighing breeze and the sunlight, listening to the confined voices from inside the synagogue, trying to pick out the voices of his father and his brother; until the day waned and the sun sank beneath the trees and the men came out of the synagogue between where they sat against the tree and the red sunset, so that the people walking by were like silhouettes without form or substance, and they hardly recognized the father when he finally came out to them.

CHAPTER FOURTEEN

He looked forward to watching television now. It was something to fix on, a miniature passion he almost consciously cultivated. It was as though he existed only on a thin layer of his consciousness, like someone who no longer needs, indeed is fearful of a large house that was once full of people, and who now, all alone, closes off the frightful emptiness to dwell in one small room.

Just inside the front door, still in his dirty clothes, he opened the newspaper to the entertainment page. He squinted at the small columns of tiny type, not just because the lenses of his glasses were dirty but because he hadn't been to the eye doctor in two years and might never go now that there was no one to prod him.

" 'Badge 714,' 'San Francisco Beat,' 'Bat Masterson,' 'Boxing,' " he murmured, mapping his way through the evening. " 'To be announced,' " he read curiously, repeated it speculatively, intrigued by that cryptic phrase. " 'To be announced . . .' "

He went through the instinctive motions of cleaning up and eating and washing the dishes. But only when he was ready to go into the living room to the television did his manner become animated, his eyes awake with that spurious animation. He didn't allow himself to realize that it was not a life line which would have implied a relationship to life, but rather an ironic reflection of real things, like those tiny landscapes one surprises in a fragment of broken glass. Realization dwelled in those closed-off rooms. He wanted no part of it and so, apparently secure in the tiny apartment he maintained in himself, he was able to live fully his microscopic life. He could even smile, as he did now, in anticipation of the Easter-egg scenes, the flat, black-and-white dramas awaiting him, the small replicas of people hidden in the maze of tubes and wires just waiting for the powerful act of his hand on the controls of the set.

But just as he flicked the knob, the telephone rang in the kitchen. With a little sigh of impatience he went to answer it.

"Yes," he demanded, bending to look through the doorway at the screen breaking into light.

"It's me, Daddy, Ruthie."

"I know."

"Did you have a good day? Work hard?"

"You know, regular."

"My Marvin had a slight fever today."

"So, you had the doctor?" Marvin, Marvin. The name, dropped into his cosy little numbness for a moment, gave him just the briefest ache before he dispelled it in his study of the screen, which now showed the brutal face of a well-known actor who played the part of a policeman in plain clothes.

"No, it wasn't too high, and by supper it was gone. I think it must be one of those bugs going around."

"Must be," Berman said listlessly, watching the car, with the policeman in plain clothes inside, roar out onto the highway, its siren whining like a toy. The policeman was talking over his car radio. Berman felt an irritation at not being able to hear what he said.

"Daddy, I bought a beautiful piece of middle chuck, just the kind you always liked. Will you come for dinner tomorrow night?"

"I can't," he said, cupping his free ear to listen to the television voice.

"Why not?"

"Why not," he echoed. "Because . . . because I . . . I don't feel so hot."

"Daddy," she said in a concerned voice.

"It's nothing, probably one of them bugs. I'll just . . ." His voiced trailed off as he thought he heard something provoking from the mouth of the gangster-looking guy who stood in the shadows outside a family's kitchen with his partner, evil figures threatening the nice-looking family in the house.

"Is someone there with you?" she asked curiously, puzzled at the vague tone of his voice.

He looked down at the telephone in his hand and it was as though he had just remembered the conversation with his daughter.

"What did you say?"

"I said, is there someone there with you?"

"No, of course not," he answered angrily, not sure if his anger came from the question or from his impatience to get to the television. "There is no one with me. I am alone."

"Do you know, you worry me. You act so strange, so *distant*. I get the feeling that you don't even want to talk to me. I feel something is happening to you, I imagine all sorts of things. I couldn't stand it if anything happened to you, I just couldn't take it after Mother. Daddy, Daddy, for God's sake have pity on me. . . ." She began crying into his ear but when he took the phone away from his head and held it down in front of him, it was like no more than the stiff little wail of a child's doll when you move it around and it says, "Waaa-aaa-aaahh."

"Stop crying, Ruthie," he said in a dull, heedless voice, shutting out the draft that had suddenly swept in from those unused rooms. "I'm all right, you're all right, everything will work itself out. Go sit down, relax with your husband, get a good night's sleep. You'll feel better in the morning."

"Dad-eee," she squealed into the phone. But he hung it back on its cradle and cut that tiny cry off. For just a moment he studied the black shape of the telephone, not really thinking of anything, rather decompressing half-consciously as though from one atmosphere to another, letting even the faint memory of the voice on the phone dwindle away until the voices from the living room usurped enough of his attention, and he walked into the living room to where he could hear the television better.

In the middle of a gun fight on a Western street, the picture began jumping, skipping frames so it was like a series of animated slides.

"Christ sake," he muttered, and got up to fuss lovingly with the controls until he corrected the picture. Then he went back to his chair to gaze with an added sense of proprietary pleasure, like a father who has picked up his toddling child after a little tumble and now watches him walk again on his baby legs.

Once, during the prize fights, when his gaze had become a little fixed and he was aware of nothing for a time, he suddenly had a feeling that he was in a horse-drawn wagon and that there were stars overhead. He even seemed to hear the clopping hoofbeats and the creak of the wheels. And then there was a din as of many voices in excitement and a cold fear in him. Emotions coursed through him, one after the other in lightning review, so that he was unable to find their shape. He shook his head violently, and, taking off his glasses, rubbed at his eyes. His head silenced and he went back to watching the fight, recalling the peculiar disturbance as only a faint ringing in his ears.

Later, when he was almost ready for bed, his body feeling

safely fatigued, his eyes heavy from the study of the flickering
screen, he said aloud, "No, that trip to Kiev was another time."
And then he frowned in bewilderment, wondering why he had
said that, a little disturbed even at that sudden, involuntary cry.

At first Berman didn't notice anything strange about the Street
of the Butchers. Walking by his father's side, holding the huge
man's hand, he was reduced to a trance of pride. Maybe two or
three times a year he was able to walk down the street *with* his
father, that is to say not three or four paces behind him, walking beside his brother and his mother while the man walked
ahead, hands behind him, head bent forward in contemplation.
On this occasion his father had taken him to buy shoes and
then started back through the Street of the Butchers. Berman
watched every face they passed for that look of awe and respect
his father spread with his presence, and it was as though something great was transmuted to even the thin, twelve-year-old
boy, so that he was stricken with joy and had eyes for none of
the small aspects of unease.

For some time he failed to notice how few people were in
the streets. None of the Jewish peddlers or stall women were
there and half the shops were closed and shuttered. Even in
those butcher shops still open there was an air of desertion,
and flies clustered undisturbed around the chickens hanging de-
nuded and headless in front of the shops.

Only when his father stopped before one of the Christian
butchers did Berman realize that their footfalls sounded loud
on the cobbled street.

The butcher, a stout, purple-faced peasant named Grigor,
hissed furtively from his doorway.

"Hey, Reb Berman," he called, beckoning with both meaty
hands.

The red-bearded man moved slowly toward the nervously gesturing man.

"I just heard from my cousin Pyotr. . . . It's in the wind."

Berman's father looked quizzically at the butcher, not really puzzled, for he understood immediately and was merely questioning the authority of the purple-faced man's warning.

The butcher nodded emphatically, looking cautiously up and down the street.

"There's no question about it. Pyotr saw the men of Dobna with his own eyes. They had sticks and torches and they were yelling, 'Dolmyk, to Dolmyk.' Just look at the street, Reb Berman," Grigor said, waving at the emptiness.

The April sunlight lay over the wooden buildings and flashed in the puddles, which were as motionless as glass. A cat walked nervously into the center of the roadway and then, taking heart in the stillness, arched its back and began walking with lordly tread, disdaining the sparrows who splashed in a little gathering of water.

"It's gotten around, no question. You know how they get sometimes around Easter," he said apologetically. "They're fools." But not he, not Grigor, he reminded by inference. He did much better being on the good side of the Jews, those feeble, cheek-turning people of such marvelous resiliency, such amazing memory. "You'd do well to get to wherever it is you folks hide, tell the others, tell them old Grigor passed the word along." He smiled fawningly at the huge, bearded Jew and it could be seen that his respect for this particular one was sincere and based on fear. "You've been good to me, Reb Berman. One hand washes the other."

"You'll not be forgotten," the big man said coldly, taking the boy's hand and turning back the way they had come in order to take the shortest route home.

And in turning they faced the menacing figure of a swarthy peasant who leaned against the wheel of a standing wagon.

Berman's father stopped for just a minute to study the man, and with pounding heart Berman gazed at the man's hard, hairy face, his eyes like small black pebbles, staring at them drunkenly. In his hand he held, loosely, a short, homemade whip.

After that brief, level appraisal, his father began to walk again, his eyes down on the cobbles in his usual attitude, his face studious and calm as always.

Berman realized he had been holding his breath when he heard the dull whack on his father's back, and he let it out with a moan as he saw the dust fly up from his father's coat. The second crack of the whip caught his father as he was half-turned, and etched a red welt under his ear.

"Ey, Jew, Christ-killer, devourer of Christian babies. Down, down on your knees . . . beg for your salvation. Pray to Him you murdered. Ey, Jew, down, down!"

"Stop, stop," the red-bearded man shouted, his face lowering with rage and yet remote from physical violence, so that his expression was not unlike the one he wore when he chastised his own children. He held his hands up in pedagogic reproof, which somehow struck Berman as being ridiculous. It made his own fear increase to see his father make that foolish gesture, as though the edifice his life was built on were toppling over to leave him defenseless.

The peasant snarled an ugly sound that might have been laughter. Then he snapped his wrist again and the whip, which Berman had thought was short, revealed its sinister length in a savage darting that left blood on his father's brow.

Berman began to cry. Through his tears he could see Grigor hiding in his shop, looking apprehensively out at the scene in the street, unwilling to be seen by either Jew or peasant, for he wished to show no allegiance he could be held accountable for. There seemed something terribly shameful to Berman in their situation, there in the daylit street for anyone to see, and the shame almost usurped his terror.

Now his father was walking toward the peasant, his hands still held high, his face hardly angry, only disapproving, stern. Couldn't he see . . .

"You must stop that! Stop, foolish man," he rumbled at the peasant.

But the peasant only swung the whip more viciously, and it caught the big Jew across his nose, leaving a wide red line there.

And then his father was next to the peasant, too close for him to use his whip easily. He raised his great, white-dusted hand and brought it down at an angle so it struck the peasant on the temple. The peasant's body seemed to fall apart, fell off aslant to the ground. His head hit the iron-shod wheel and seemed cloven in two; the blood spread suddenly over the ground and ran into the puddles of dirty water.

Reb Berman looked dazedly at his hand, then down at the motionless figure of his tormentor. "Lord forgive me, I was sorely pressed. Thus be it."

Grigor darted out from the door of his shop to kneel at Berman's feet as he examined the fallen peasant. Berman could see the waxy roots of the butcher's hair, the brown stains of dried pig blood on his shoulders. The street was still empty. The great, red-bearded man stood silently beside the boy, looking down, the expression of his eyes hidden in the shadows of his jutting brows.

"Whew-w-w," Grigor exclaimed. "It's all up with him, Reb Berman! You did him in and that's the God's truth. Oh, my, look at that head . . . broke like an egg! You're a powerful man." He looked up at the motionless Jew as though hoping to surprise some fear, some expression of abjection or at least request. But there was nothing on that massive face except overpowering dignity, so he sighed and shrugged as he scanned the street carefully. "It's safe with me, Reb Berman. I saw nothing . . . nothing."

Berman's father nodded slowly. Then he took his son's hand

and began walking back the way they had come, his footsteps sounding heavy, one to every two or three of the boy's, down the empty street that was so still you could hear the flies buzzing in the April sunshine.

And there was a time, a time of surging glory for the boy, a series of moments when a strange magic was in him, so he thought he felt the presence of God in unique vestments and the world was filled with a peculiar singing mystery as he walked hand in hand with his father down the deserted Street of the Butchers.

It was cool at dusk that evening. There was a presentiment of fall in the hazy air and he stood for a few minutes on the sidewalk, looking both ways up the street. The trees were in heavy leaf, dark green, burdened with the last of their youth. An ache of poignancy seeped through the numbness of his age, and he sighed and looked up at the house, which seemed to rear up like a mausoleum.

In a bewildered murmur he told himself that it got worse instead of better, that instead of healing, his wound seemed to quicken as though the anesthesia he had sought to create were wearing off. He shuddered at the thought of what the pain could develop into. Then he forced himself up the steps and into the house.

But once he was inside a change came over him. He no longer saw himself with that sad objectivity. Of late he seemed to hover just over the past, sometimes dropping into it for a minute or two in the middle of something he was doing, so that right after he would gaze around and wonder where he was. It made for a confusion that showed in the conversations he had on the telephone with his daughter, and, as a result, more and more she pressed her suit on him. Her increasing desperation for him only served to thrust him still more deeply into that trip through the hours in the house which now was like nothing so much as a roller-coaster route that descended into different levels of time, culminating in the dark when he lay on his bed and lived in his most remote history, smiling sometimes, crying, murmuring words to himself—an old man, lost to his body and the horrid anger of his bereavement.

And sometimes, even in his active, fully awake hours, his reminiscences had a continuity that carried over from one brief visitation of lost time to the next. The occasional visitors he had remarked with pity and concern the absent, darting look of his eyes, which made it seem he maintained the conversation with them only out of the smallest obligations of courtesy, while his deepest attention was focused on some puzzling middle distance.

So it was on that cool evening, when he washed his upper body at the sink, that while the water ran he lost himself in the sensation of riding in a horse-drawn wagon, saw faces of people he had known only in a glimpse a half-century before. Bearded men, youths with white, sweaty, consumptive faces, old women with faces browned and dried down to that age where men and women look the same, standing behind their stalls of fruits and vegetables the like of which Berman had never encountered again—apples, plums, pears, squashes, radishes, eggplants, all possessed of that peerless taste with which his youthful tongue had endowed them. The wagon rocked over the broken paving stones, tossing his brother against him, and they mauled each other in mock anger until the gigantic figure on the driver's seat turned his red-bearded frown on them and they subsided into furtive giggles, while Berman watched the onion-shaped church towers moving by against the Russian sky. And they had sweetmeats while the father supervised the loading of great sacks of sugar and salt and flour into the back of the wagon. While the white dust flew from the roughly handled sacks, making the wagon look clouded like a magic vehicle, Berman heard the loud, long-drawn invitation of the ice-cream peddler. *"Sacha-neema-roj, sacha-neema-roj . . ."* And the father, making a great show of unsmiling severity, opened his snap-top purse, and the man carrying a keg on his head stopped without further signal and served up chunks of the strawberry ice cream, working with the cups on the little counter on his chest. Then the father just nodded once at their expectant faces and they took the cups and the long-handled wooden spoons and fed their mouths that unimaginable bliss in the autumn afternoon, while the flour made a white mist around their father.

"Sacha-neema-roj," Berman said tenderly to the old, spectacled face. Until he saw it was his own and cursed at the water slopping over the sides of the sink, the din of it rushing out of the gleaming faucet. He shut it off, let the water run down the drain, mopped up the floor with the little netted rag that always lay in the elbow of the pipe under the sink. Once while he was down on his hands and knees he felt his mouth twist into that dreamy smile, but he recovered himself and moved more quickly to get what he was doing finished.

The rabbi of the synagogue he and his family had attended for many years stopped by to see him that night. Berman let him in with a little grunt of intended civility, motioned him to a chair, and sat down himself, a blandly courteous expression on his face.

"I meant to stop by sooner, Mr. Berman. It's been on my mind ever since . . . your terrible loss," the man with the gold-rimmed spectacles said, his mouth small under the neat mustache, his voice professionally sonorous and rich. "I have worried about you, all of us have. But at times like this your friends can offer great comfort. Why haven't you come down to see us?" At the lack of response from the big, expressionless face, he went on, thinking perhaps the man was still too distracted by his grief to think clearly. "I know you as a religious man, Mr. Berman. Over the years you have been devoted to your religion. Don't you think that now is the time when your faith can be of the greatest solace? I was very surprised, upset even, to find you absent all this time. You have never been to the shul, nor have your children, for the memorial services— not even that." Now his face took on a harassed expression; he had the feeling he was talking to a dummy, and he had to wipe delicately at his mustache as though to reassure himself. "Mr. Berman, you must realize that God, in His infinite wisdom, can be of the greatest consolation."

Berman just shook his head.

The rabbi was startled, as if he had begun to get used to that lifeless demeanor and was shocked at the sudden, emphatic life in that negating movement of Berman's head.

"Mr. Berman, surely you have not succumbed to bitterness, to hopelessness. You must realize that God's ways are not to be understood by us. He . . ."

"Don't bother me with Him, Rabbi."

"How can you say that! He is with you always, there is no denying Him. Oh, Mr. Berman, you are not doing yourself any good being bitter at God. He has reasons. We are but made in His image, not in His wisdom. He has ways that . . ."

"What He has done to me all my life and now this . . . He is my enemy. I see His face in my nightmares, the joke he has played on me. It makes the whole thing a stupidity, a terrible stupidity, without reason. I prayed, I was good to my neighbors, my family. I never hurt a living soul if I could help it. And what has He given me? What!"

"Have you read the book of Job, Mr. Berman? There is a lesson in it for all of us. God tested Job, tried him more than any man. . . ."

"I read it. It's a joke. Like any stupid man He tried to show off to the Devil, to prove He was stronger. Such nonsense . . .

If it is true it only makes what I say all the more right—that He is cruel and takes pleasure in demonstrating how powerful He is, like Superman. 'See what I can do!' "

"Oh, no, Mr. Berman, you miss the entire point of . . ."

But Berman wasn't listening now, although the rabbi took heart from the suddenly gentle look on his face, and began to speak more eloquently and confidently.

"It is written that . . ."

Night had begun to fall as they left the environs of Kiev. Berman and his brother lay sprawled in the back of the wagon, much higher now on the piles of flour and sugar sacks his father had bought for the bakery. Around his mouth there was a stickiness from the ice cream and he ran his tongue over his lips, searching for the residue of sweetness. As they left the city they passed the peasants driving animals the other way toward the markets in Kiev, and the smell of sheep and dust mingled with the scent of fallen leaves and trampled grapes and bruised, odorous apples. And then it was dark, with the cries of the shepherds gone from the air. He looked up and was dizzied by the great well of the heavens, the stars sprayed across it as from some gigantic explosion, caught motionless on their flight outward by the brevity of his vision. And larger still, seated beside the dim shape of his mother, the great figure of his father, swaying to the motion of the wagon so it seemed he prayed, so similar was his aspect to that of his swaying morning devotions. And the stars in the sky were like the lights of a great city as the wagon swayed, and Berman abided in fantastic happiness. . . .

Until the rabbi's face loomed before him, voiceless at first in spite of his working mouth, as though a wall of silence separated them. And Berman scowled at the present, standing in the midst of the rabbi's words.

" '. . . *anue,*' which, translated means, 'God is the Giver.' "

"Enough, Rabbi, you have nothing for me," Berman interrupted. "There's no more to be said."

"Mr. Berman, I wish you would relent, listen to . . ."

"I appreciate you coming, Rabbi. It was nice of you."

The rabbi got up with a sigh and followed Berman to the door. His face was troubled and he felt shaken to such a degree that he knew he would not even relate this failure to his wife.

"Please try to order your thoughts, Mr. Berman. There is something in your attitude that makes me concerned over your . . . your health. . . ."

Berman laughed, a short, harsh sound.

"You mean my mind. You think I might be losing my mind. Well-l-l-l . . ." His face was cruel, malicious, as he seemed to consider that possibility. "It's possible, it could be."

Then he closed the door gently but firmly on the rabbi and stood leaning against it, listening to the man's descent of the porch steps, and finally—after a moment, as though the rabbi had stood uncertain about direction—to his footfalls sounding on the sidewalk, diminishing until they were lost to Berman's hearing.

When he lay on the bed later, he allowed the familiar lassitude that was the climate for his dreaming; but there was a scornful, sardonic smile on his mouth, too, as though he said in thought to that malicious Creator, "Go on, feed me those daydreams, even those won't get me. I don't know what's up your sleeve with those dreams. But for now, they pass the time anyhow."

September, 1907

He must have been sleeping, for the sky had paled near the horizon and his eyes were sticky with sleep in the chill air. Yet so slumberous was the ride with the swaying of the wagon and the steady thudding of the horses' hoofs, so close to dream was his reception of the world in that comforting rhythm, that there was no transition between sleeping and waking, no boundary to cross that could mark his degree of consciousness. His brother was a lumpy form, completely covered by the blanket they had been sharing. Above and in front the figures of his parents rocked against the dawning sky. His mother was sleeping with her head on his father's shoulder, but his father sat straight, the red hair bright in the gray light before day.

It was some time that he lay thus, unwilling to move, as though sudden movement could break that abiding somnolence, trusting to the rhythm and the feel of the ride. But when he saw the first warm red in the sky, he heard the rushing voice of the river, suddenly very close as though it had held a silence at their approach, waiting to thunder at them so they would give it attention and not relegate it to a mere sound of the landscape.

Berman sat up then on the bags of flour to peer through the morning ground fog for the first sight of the river. He saw the dewy tops of the long wild grasses, the broad limbs of old oaks and beech trees, stationary in the uncertain light, like giants muted by the coming of day; and beyond, the groves of blue-green pines and spruces which he knew bordered the river. Then it appeared, a broad, living reflection of the lightening sky, merged with the shore on its edges where it mirrored distortedly the pines and spruces; and its sound up close was soft, yet so all-embracing that it gave an impression of great volume, like a whisper from a titan's throat.

The road followed along it now, and Berman timed the small floating sticks and leaves, trying to judge the velocity and the speed of the river, yet sensing all the time that the real power and movement were underneath that flat, reflecting surface, beyond his ability to measure or even guess at.

The road began to show familiar landmarks now: a hunter's

stone hut, the ancient manor house with its avenue of elms, the potato field that was just out of sight of Dolmyk.

A boat appeared on the broad current. A peasant and a boy were bent over a net as their boat pulled against the anchoring rope. Suddenly they pulled the net up into the boat, tumbling a confusion of silver. The man looked toward the wagon rumbling along the deserted dawn road. He called out something in a hoarse voice. Then he held a fish aloft in his hand, a shape of brief sparkle and brilliance.

Berman gasped as though transfixed by something beyond naming. His little sound brought the father's head around, eyes red rimmed from the night of looking at darkness. Berman pointed as though in apology toward the man holding the fish aloft on the river. His father followed his gesture, studied the simple sight with an expression of perplexity as though he had just come back from a vastly different consideration. Finally he turned back to his son. They held their eyes locked for just a few seconds, both puzzled now in the gently rocking wagon with the other boy and the woman asleep and only the two of them awake in that morning light. Until finally the father nodded slowly at the boy, confirming something wondrous to him, something he would have all the time in the world to find out.

August, 1956

"Oh, no, I'm through with you. No man is supposed to take all this," Berman muttered, eyes streaming in the darkness of the bedroom. "Nothing, absolutely nothing you can do will make me stop hating you, your cruelness, your . . ."

And then he stopped, sat up in the bed in shocked surprise. It suddenly had occurred to him that no one heard him, that he was talking to himself. In absolute emptiness.

CHAPTER SIXTEEN

There was a deep perplexity in him now that haunted him to the exclusion even of anger, and his waking hours were as filled with the confusion of time as his dreams in bed.

Riebold watched him with a guardian sorrow during the day, for he was of little use on the job, likely to stand over a small chore, wrench in hand, staring at the air as though before some monumental decision.

"Yussel," Riebold would interpose gently. "Let me have the wrench. The water is shut off, the people are without water. Let me do it."

And Berman would raise his furrowed, suffering face in bewilderment, would look from the tool in his hand to his partner and then out at the day, as though wondering where he was now, in what form he inhabited the earth.

"What is it, did you ask me something?" he might ask, his voice phlegmy and ancient.

"No, no," Riebold would answer comfortingly, as to a child. He would take the wrench from his partner's hand, patting him lightly on the shoulder as he turned away, a gesture that tried to implant safety and reassurance. He just wanted Berman to stay where he was, felt at least keeping him in the one *physical* place was a delaying action against the dark forces that showed in his friend's eyes.

So Berman might stand in the reality of the late summer sunlight and hear things that were out of hearing, see shapes that were transparent, while only a few feet away the bearlike Riebold labored in the present; and he would be in both places and suffering at the great mystery put upon him. . . .

The father was huge and stern in his rusty beard. There was no fun or play with him. It was a harsh hour to be left in the house with him while the mother went to the market to shop. No pal, no warm friend was he, that brooding man unaccustomed to his children. For a while he stared at the two boys, restless under his gaze, which was dark and disapproving of their laziness, an offense to Him. "Let me hear your lessons," he finally said, in the room that was quiet except for the bubbling hiss of the samovar. And Berman recited in the droning, unfeeling way of his rudimentary learning, hearing the sounds from the river outside, deprived, miserable. And yet . . .

His son-in-law had once got into a discussion with Berman several years before.

"All right, Pa, sure, you had respect for your father, I can see that. I play on the floor with my kids, I'm more familiar with them. We're *closer* to our children today. Love. Maybe less respect, but love." The young man had sat back in his chair a little smugly. Suddenly he leaned forward, smiling to deliver the *coup de grâce*. "But tell me this. You were afraid of your father, you respected him, sure. But did you really have any other feeling for him? Tell the truth, now."

And very simply yet with such shattering force did Berman answer that his son-in-law looked down in embarrassment, unable to countenance that terrible disclosure from the usually undramatic, stolid, fifty-five-year-old plumber.

"I adored him," Berman had said. . . .

Somehow the days were got through, though at great cost to

Riebold. He would tap his partner on the shoulder and nod toward the truck, trying to make of the day something normal and mutual.

"We did enough today, Yussel. Come, let's pack it in, hah? There's always tomorrow."

And Berman would look around him and finally nod, perhaps convinced by his partner's kindly fraud. He would wonder where the day had gone, would say as much to Riebold, shaking his head as though with the normal regret of men his age.

"I tell you, Leo, I'm getting old. You know, I hardly even remember what we did today. I'm getting *s'misht,* foggy in my old age." He would try to put a chuckle in it, but in a few minutes, as they rode along in the truck, he would be lost in that vacant gaze again, deaf to the pipes rattling in the back of the truck and his partner's pitying sighs beside him.

Then home to the television, which had become only an obligation toward numbness, for lately even that superficial peace was beyond him.

He sat before the animated screen but his attention was broken by a restlessness, a nervousness, as though something waited just beyond his ken, something to be recognized. In and out of the reveries he darted, hunting through the layers of time for—what?—a reason for his sudden sense of emptiness . . . his sudden loss of that vital anger. His daughter, beside herself with anxiety for him, he turned off, hung up in the middle of her pleas. Once his son-in-law came over, determined for his wife's peace of mind to bring the old man to her way of thinking.

"Look, Pa, this can't go on," he said firmly. "I'm going to have to insist that you pack up and come to us. Ruth is just going out of her mind about you. I can see why; you're not acting right. For Christ sake, you're building up to a breakdown if you keep on like this."

But Berman had stood up and gone over to the younger man, mighty and inflexible even in his age and distraction.

"I'll come, I'll come, when I'm ready. You just go home to her, tell her everything will turn out."

So that, defeated as always by that unwordy man who never gave you an argument you could come to grips with, the son-in-law had gone and left Berman to his evening of television and strange musings.

He watched the miniature events on the screen and groped backward and forward in time, for the sense of it. . . .

From the house the pines were a blue-green screen for the black river. He stood on its banks sometimes, breathed in regretfully the scent of the bitter river mud, the Russian earth, wild flowers blended in like part of the recipe with the frail smell of his mother's bread. His mother was calling him, sending her voice querulously over the outdoor sounds. Slowly he took leave for the while of his pointy face, water-combed by the rushing river, wondering how a person could live any other place if not by a river. The land went north to Kiev and Petrograd with the water still. Or you could put a chip on the mud-clouded surface to watch the heart go south to the Sea of Azov and the Black Sea and beyond. . . .

But here, by some ugly and unimportant miracle, gray faces performed in his living room, and he was old and lonely watching them, night after night, waiting for some sort of—what?— "To be announced"? People laughed on the screen. He searched for the joke in their smooth faces, needed the sight of them . . . an anchor . . . from which he could delve into himself, carve with exquisite pain the tender organ of his memory. . . .

Sometimes he would leave the dusty taste of the cheder behind him, all the vowels and consonants of the old tongue, to go to the river edge, there to watch the rushing past, watch desperately with all his might. Some drop of water was fleeing forever between the rank shores, smelling of rushes and the ancient mud. He stood in the river wind, ear locks blown impiously, damp vellum of the schoolbook forgotten in his hand, to watch the Christian peasants netting blue fishes—bright, clear creatures like the blue transparency of fire. His teeth chilled delightfully in his open smile. There was thrumming inside his head, inside the brain-tight *yamalka,* silk-embroidered, his father's austere gift from a trip to Kiev in the spring of his birth. He stood, daring his father's anger, knee deep in the sinful, velvet mud. Above was the Ukrainian morning-shine, beneath, the hidden urging of the cold river against his chilled legs. And the sun carried the flow into the gold of distance, blue and gold there like riches just out of reach. . . .

Ah, but here the people were dancing in a ballroom in long gowns whose color you had to imagine from the gray tones— a waltz . . . ta tum te tum . . . until this guy has to stop it to tell about this cleaner in a bottle, this miracle cleaner that cleans your walls, your car, your dog; maybe your soul, too? . . .

From the depths of his feather bed on summer evenings, he heard the river singing. Entwined somehow with his father's deep, bearded voice and the high, soft plea of his mother's comfort, and the restlessness of his brother rustling the awkward age. Heard voices, barbarous voices in the summer twilight from his bed of ineffable comfort. Sighed and dreamed great shapeless dreams, felt sleep coming like an older friend, delivering him along valuable hours. . . .

Whata they got here now, a rocket or something. *Whoosh,* fast . . . Where is it going? Up, how high, to the moon, some crazy place. What do they want to go there? How high do they got to go . . . for what? This guy is explaining . . . who can make head or tail?

He sat on the edge of his chair, leaning into the microscopic warmth of the screen. It was the only infinitesimal piece to the dizzying puzzle. He could not lose that. A little rabbit was telling him to buy . . .

Suddenly the screen went black.

Desperately he got up and went around to the back of the

set. Curses tumbled from his mouth and his hands were shaking. He tore off the cardboard backing to stare in bewilderment at the maze of wires and tubes there. At first he touched lightly, tentatively, at some of the most harmless-looking shapes—a screw, a little plastic-coated wire. Then he began more frantically tugging at wires and tubes. A panic came over him at the lifelessness of the mechanism. Just by his wild groping he hoped to breathe life into it. Sweat broke out on his body, chilled on him. His heart pounded audibly.

Suddenly ferocious life snaked up his arm and reached for his heart. He gave a loud cry as the electricity shot through him. He felt himself thrown, as though by a gigantic hand, down to the floor. Stunned, he lay there. He didn't know if he could move, refused to try.

In the emptiness he began to cry, a simple, childlike weeping. Then, because there was nothing else, because his thoughts and his grievances were amputated for the moment, and he was left only with some of the old reflexes of the spirit, he began to moan:

"*Baruch atah Adonoi* . . . God in Heaven . . . Mary, Mary, my wife . . . forgive me. . . . *V'yiskadash* . . . *Gott in Himmel* . . . forgive me. . . ."

He wished with all his heart not to die there on the living-room floor, so senselessly, with no chance to make a little peace with himself.

In a mingling of the languages he had spoken in his life, English, Russian, Yiddish, he prayed without realizing he prayed, begged with no memory of pride, to come out of that living death he had made for himself, to be touched by life again; and his words were short, strangled sounds that fell back on him in the dusty, cloistered room with all the tiny delicacies, the miniature mementos of the life lived there.

Until, with a deep sense of shock and amazement, he realized he was not hurt. And that no one listened to him, that for all he could ever comprehend, there was only emptiness. For the first time in his life he knew, as he hadn't known even in his deepest despair and rage, that there was no Enemy, no Betrayer, no bearded Torturer; and for a minute or two that knowledge froze him in a fearful grief that made all the other suffering like a child's peevishness beside it. He was alone. How could death measure up to that blackness!

So when he finally got up from the floor and stepped carefully over the litter of tubes and wires he had strewn there, he was conscious of a greater courage than had ever existed in him before. All by himself he went to the front door and opened it. No one watched him do it, no one molested him. He went out on the porch. A man and woman went by talking. The woman laughed. He pitied them. Could he call that dry, calm feeling peace? It didn't matter.

A peculiar craving came over him . . . not for food. He found himself trying to drink in the street, the people who strolled by, the ground, the stars. Idly, almost without feeling at all but with a weary curiosity, he wondered how he had become that mournful old man when such a short time before he had been invincibly young.

But the street would give him no answer, so he just stood there, breathing in the sweet, cool air, smelling the conglomerate scents, hearing the million tiny sounds as little more than a ringing in his ears. Peace, was this the peace?

After a while he went into the house, past the litter of tubes and wires on the floor, through the cushioned rooms, past the empty bedrooms.

He knew just that he was very tired, that he would sleep. He wondered heedlessly, as he lay on his bed, whether he would die then from merely an absence of will.

Yet in the dark, miraculously, he heard it.

Heard it in the crevice between day and sleep—the river, singing that one glorious monotony. It left him forever yet always arrived again. He woke to it in the morning, under the blackened wooden ceiling. It was as great as the sound of his father's harsh morning prayers, more and less, too, than that bass voice crying *"Adonoi."* Yet part of it, too, like the bread smell, was wedded to the river scent.

"So what, what is it all about?" he asked in his old man's American bed. And he realized that he was not through with it, that he had at least a little of the answer to find.

CHAPTER SEVENTEEN

August, 1956

The question buzzed in Berman's head like the very voice of the heat. He got out of bed slowly, noticing the shine on his rarely sweating skin. For a moment he stared in bewilderment at the wide-open windows. He tried to relate his curious sense of quest with this morning that had no breeze or movement. He washed his body, and dressed in a clean sport shirt and crisp khaki pants, trying all the while to reduce that distraction of the heat; until, suddenly, as he stood in the kitchen squaring his Panama hat on his head, the heat became relevant to his questioning attitude. He looked at the open kitchen windows vaguely.

"It's a hot day," he mumbled. "A scorcher. Ah, well . . ."

Almost dreamily he dialed his daughter's number. The clock showed seven fifteen as he waited out the buzzes. "Sleeping yet."

"Oh, Daddy, you woke me up. Are you all right? What time is it? *Seven fifteen!* What's wrong, why are you calling so early?" Her voice was hoarse and sleepy in the receiver and Berman held it a little away from his ear.

"Only that I'm going out now."

"You're going to work . . . well, okay, but I'll be expecting you this afternoon as usual. What time?"

"No, Ruthie, I'm not coming today," he said.

"You're working *all day.* Oh, Daddy, it's going to be awfully hot. . . . Please don't work all day."

"No, no, I'm not working at all today."

"Well, I don't understand then."

"I have things to do."

"What in the world could you have that would take a whole Saturday? At least you'll have supper . . ."

"No supper."

"Daddy," she complained. "You aren't making sense. Oh, I have a good mind to send Bob over and force you . . ."

"There's no explaining," Berman said. "I'll talk to you to-night or tomorrow." Then he hung up on her hoarse, worried voice.

As he stepped outside, readjusting the butter-colored Panama, he began to examine the day carefully. The trees could have been the oddities in a glass ball, their greenery graven in the heat, without a hint of life in their motionless leaves. Nothing moved in his view. No birds exploded from the clustered branches, no cats snaked across the fences. The grass stood as lifeless as a well-worn rug, and two hard-white clouds were fastened in the pale blue above him. His slow breathing seemed a prodigious act, a great defiance in the heat.

What was this, anyhow—a pilgrimage? He thought with mild amusement of the religious men in Russia who traveled great distances to visit some miracle rabbi. Then he had to shrug, because he wasn't sure that his aimlessness made any sense. All he knew was that sometime between the previous night and this morning there had begun this odd momentum. So that, at one point, he had decided not to work that day. And that subtle decision had led to his dressing in the clean clothes of leisure and some other moment had brought him far enough to tell his

daughter he would not visit her that day and still another moment shaped the message to Riebold, even as Riebold was carefully parking the truck in front of the house.

"You're all dressed up," Riebold said in amazement.

"I'm not going to work today, Leo. Go on without me."

"How come, Yussel? What is it you have to do?" The big,
bearish face was framed comically in the truck window, awed
at the immaculate splendor of his partner. Riebold looked down
uneasily at his own work clothes, as though he suddenly considered the possibility of his having overlooked some holiday.

"Nothing to tell about. I'm taking a holiday is all. Gonna loaf
around by myself," Berman said, with a faint Mona Lisa smile.

"All of a sudden. Okay, sure, you could use a rest. . . .
But I don't know, Yussel, you got a shit-eatin' look about you.
Do you feel all right?"

"Don't worry," Berman said, breaking into a genuine smile.
"I have some personal business."

"You're sure you're not going to do something crazy, Yussel?
I don't like the way you've been acting lately," Riebold said
peevishly, his heavy face wrinkled with worry and curiosity.
"I mean, you want to take the day off, fine. But you got to tell
me what you're gonna do; I got a right to know!"

"Mind your own business, Leo," Berman said gently. "Anyhow, the truth is that I'm not sure. . . . Only that I feel like
wandering around. What will be, I don't know. What I'll ac-
complish"—he shrugged—"no one can know." He spoke in a
bemused, soft voice and his glasses caught the burning light
through the trees; his eyes were hidden again from his friend
and Riebold could only sigh his habitual sense of helplessness
and confusion.

"Yussel, Yussel, Yussel," he said sadly from the window of
the truck. Then, for a minute or two longer he stared intensely
at Berman, as though he saw his friend's figure receding even
now before the truck moved. And when he finally started the

motor and rolled slowly away, he sighed in accompaniment to the gnashing gears as he rode his careful way down the street.

Even then, when Berman was alone in the street with certain bridges burned behind him, his plans extended only to the most immediate moments ahead. Yet even in that fogged foresight he felt confident that he would get out of the day all that was in it.

As he walked through the rising heat of early morning, he was without emotional memory. Everything that had happened to him was locked away someplace deep inside and all he was left with were the tiny, recorded images, reproductions of the way he had felt, not disturbing, and with no more impact than microfilm has for the naked eye. And like a lens of great and mysterious selectivity his gaze on a passing woman was as bland and depthless as a reflection.

He walked through the thick heat of the air without consciousness of distance. At times he was aware of a faint, high singing, a cricket sound, a boiling, plucked-wire note like the persistent voice of the heat. People's voices had the quality of curses, and dogs barked hopelessly, as though at a great invisible threat that made them walk backward with their hair on end. Once he stopped to note a thermometer on the corner of a building. "Only quarter to eight and already eighty-six," he said proudly, wanting extraordinary qualities for the day. He heard young girls singing somewhere out of his sight and he curved his mouth slightly. Only Berman and the children were above the heat, and the children couldn't know their gift.

Then he was downtown, standing in front of the three churches on the green. It was the place where most of the city's buses began and ended their routes. He counted seventeen blue-and-white buses that pulled up, emptied, filled again, and drove away.

The dispatcher gave a side glance of half-concealed irritation at Berman, so neat and cool-looking even in the full sun.

"What's the matter, don't we got any buses suit ya?" he said to Berman, just barely bending his mouth in his sweaty face. He was trying to keep it a joke.

"That's all right. Don't worry yourself. Something will turn up," Berman said with a faint grin.

Then a bus pulled up with the word WOODMONT over the windshield. Without a moment's hesitation Berman boarded it. From the window he gave the dispatcher a quick, condescending wink.

He didn't question or wonder at the rightness unfolding in his itinerary. Only vaguely, half-consciously, he nodded at the streets the bus rocked through, as though only an absent discretion kept him from saying, "Yes, yes, this is the way." The stone and brick of the city drank in the whitening sunlight and the people hurried from shadow to shadow as in some odd game of musical chairs, where they risked being caught when the rhythm changed. One old man stared fearfully at the sky, his sagging face hopeless yet defiant at the sight. Berman shook his head in amazement.

As the city thinned to lower buildings, houses, and one-room stores, he lowered his head to the open part of the window so that the hot wind of their passage would fan his face. He studied the burning wreckage of a junk yard, the gleaming death of a used-car lot, peered curiously at the little brown patches of grass, the children sitting in dreams in half-hidden yards, the grapevines, the boats up on scaffolds in driveways, like individual arks waiting for an impossible flood. And all the while the order and logic of the day grew on him like the outer edges of a vast puzzle he was patiently anticipating.

Then the first rank odor of salt reached him and the air turned fresher, cooler. The houses had no cellars and the few people along the road were clad in shorts or bathing suits. A glinting piece of the great surface showed between the cottages. And then there was the sea.

The bus stopped at a little plaza surrounded by stores and

cottages and Berman got out. He walked past an open fruit stand, a small hotel. Between the hotel and some bathhouses he turned abruptly to walk over the sand toward the water.

There was a little sea wall between the hotel and the sand. He sat on it and opened himself to the immense vista of the ocean, flat and sparkling and reaching to the ends of vision. The beach began to fill with people. There were small, thin boys with dark, betrayed-looking faces, who brought little traces of pain to his chest. And full-bodied, white-skinned women who carried their bodies into the shallow, lapping water as though they knew their worth. The sun rose higher in the sky. Young girls ran over the sand-bars and after them the youths with proud chests and silver religious medals against their tans. They splashed and skidded sheets of water into silvery sprays. There was laughter, and shouts that fell short and small beneath the stupendous heavens. An old woman floated her arthritic limbs on the rising tide, bobbed up and down with a beatific expression on her ancient face. People passed Berman to and from the beach and those that glanced his way only furrowed their eyes at the odd, alien look of him, hatted, buttoned up, wearing street shoes; they were unable to make out his intention, with his eyes shadowed by the brim, hidden behind the lenses.

At noon the sun was fire on his shoulders, threatening to ignite his Panama hat. People eating lunches on blankets all around glanced curiously at him and mumbled their suspicions. One of the people from the hotel, maybe the owner, came out on the porch to gaze at his back for a minute or two as though considering the idea of telling Berman to move. But he went back inside and Berman sat on, part of the landscape, a solar figure that came to be forgotten by the bathers finally, like the sea wall itself. He soaked time as the others soaked the sunlight and a bedlam was in him—tears, laughter, anger—yet all moving, circulating too fast to ruffle his face with its absent smile. The tide came full and slipped out again. Shadows grew longer from the bases of things—human beings, cottages, rocks —from each grain of sand. Yet the heat seemed, if anything, to grow more intense, more breathless.

A pain started in his deformed kidney; he hadn't moved his position on the wall for some time. It spread through him until it reached his head, where it pounded like something desperate to escape. And then it was that he sensed something malevolent in the air. He raised his head, startled at the resurgence. Could he have been wrong, might that Enemy be there after all?

A dark collar lay slyly on the circle of the horizon, retiring, falsely humble at the edge of the broad expanse of empty blue. He was so tired. He stood up as though to brace himself in the familiar defiance. The air was close against his aching head. Was there emptiness? Or that black God?

"It's going to storm tonight," a fat woman said as she looked up from her effort of folding a beach umbrella.

Berman trudged past her and the woman forgot the weather *and* the umbrella for just a moment. Something odd crossed her face so swiftly that it was apparent it would leave her mind just as quickly as it had come. Indeed it might have gone while she watched Berman's retreating back, and her eyes were on him now without memory of what she had seen on his face.

While he waited for the bus he, too, became curious about his face. There was a gum machine with a long, narrow mirror in front of the soda fountain where he waited. A strange face stared back at him from the narrow mirror, a shiny, polished-bone face with superfluous spectacles and hat brim like the grotesque joke of a costumed skeleton. He twisted his mouth to bring it to life, but before he could tell if he had succeeded, the bus snorted up to the curb behind him and he turned hurriedly to board it.

All the way back to the city he studied the sky, blind to the world of houses and trees and people below. The clouds grew more assertive, slid slowly over the fading blue. A wind came up, first in little advance puffs that lifted dust and swung it in low swirlings over the ground. When he got off the bus in downtown New Haven on the exact corner he had embarked from that morning, the wind continued with increasing violence. But there, in the center of the city, its force was manifested in the swinging of store signs and electric wires, the frivolous tampering with women's skirts, the flattening of shirts against men's chests. Like a hand, he thought, like a great, pressing hand.

People rushed in different directions, their faces hard and inward, determined on fixed destinations; they refused to look up at the closing darkness. Berman walked among them slowly, in the opposite direction from his home, and his was the only face that was raised. He saw people and buildings, but only with a sort of side vision; it was as though he stored the sight of what happened on the ground with the intention of taking out those images for later study. Now he was concerned with the renewed possibility of his Enemy.

He was walking through an old section of town, the neighborhood he had lived in with his mother and brother when he had first come to the city as a youth. Now that section of town was populated with Italians and Negroes, and there were many bars and stores. He was looking at the wind-emptied stoops and sidewalks with an absent curiosity, when suddenly the wind stopped. A great emptiness filled the world with a greenish light, and people crept outside again curiously to study the void. Berman glanced cautiously upward from time to time, guarded, suspicious, feeling the malignant Presence more tangible in the mocking stillness.

But the others, more trustful and innocent than he, ventured farther from their doorways. Children began racing through the motionless heat. Echoless noises took over the street: boys banging garbage-can covers, women laughing. Two narrow-headed adolescents, a boy and a girl, walked past him bumping their bodies together. The girl squealed foolishly at each contact and Berman turned to watch them, although his face seemed to be thinking of something else. An old woman with a huge, shapeless body and a white, melted face stopped before Berman and opened her mouth to speak to him. But then she saw his face more clearly and realized he wasn't anyone she knew, and she stepped awkwardly out of his way with a little apologetic smile. A woman sat rocking a baby. The baby was whining its sleepy discomfort and the woman murmured unintelligible assurances while she watched Berman with dark, expressionless eyes. The sky held them all, Berman and the rest of them, and for all their little motions of life they seemed like creatures caught in the dark, greenish stillness of the air.

The heat grew more intense. Everything seemed to simmer, then come to a boil in his head. "What, what," he muttered in pain, with his head facing the street and his eyes rolled back to stare upward.

Then he was passing the red glow of a tavern and there was a blast of noise. Men boiled out of the doorway and he found himself in their midst. He stopped patiently and watched without interest the two men cast in the middle of the little throng.

"Go 'head, call me a stupid wop *now!*" The speaker was a heavy, mournful-faced man with the black-rimmed eyes of a dreamer.

"You call me a dirty nigger, I call you that," the thin, yellow-skinned man said.

"You *are* a dirty nigger," the heavy man cried, driven by the crowding, eager faces.

And then they were scuffling clumsily. Fists sounded on bone and flesh occasionally, but mostly there was the sound of their feet and their furious breathing. The crowd murmured encouragement, but not too loudly, out of respect for the more meaningful sounds of the fight.

Berman stood among them, but mostly he surveyed the spectators, the few women who came up, anxious, disapproving, yet fascinated. And more of him was focused on the black, impending sky, wondering what this had to do with that.

And then, in the midst of the scuffling, murmurous people and the patient dark, there came the loud blare of a siren, and harsh, judging light approached along the street. Berman felt the crowd fray at the edges, thin and leak away. And when the light was on them, there were only a few men and women up close, and Berman, and the two combatants suddenly in a motionless embrace in the searchlight beam. The others were safely back on the steps of houses or watching from doorways. The fighters peered blindly into the glare, forgetting with their bloody faces to let go of each other; they looked as if they were very dear to each other.

"Okay, okay, what is this?" said the large, faceless figure approaching from the light. "Don't no one move. . . . Let's see what this is all about." Then the policeman was close enough so Berman could make out the harsh, clean face, the darting, analyzing eyes. The policeman's gaze searched all the men, hatless and in their undershirts, until he fixed on Berman standing sober and neat with his Panama square on his head.

"You, you with the hat, you tell me what this is about!"

Berman just waved his hand and shook his head.

"Come on now, don't give me a hard time. . . . You was a witness, let's have it!"

"A witness?" Berman said. "No, no, I'm not from around here, count me out."

"What do you mean, count you out! Shall I pretend you wasn't here at all?" the policeman said. His voice was sour and his face seemed to express more hostility to Berman than to the two fighters, who had shyly released their hold on each other and were now covering their embarrassment by fixing their gazes on Berman. "Count you out," the policeman said contemptuously. "You don't want to be involved, hah! Well, that's too bad."

Berman looked upward at the crowding dark and his mouth was fixed in a line of grim exasperation. He had the feeling he might be missing something from that apparently fathomless sky. If only the cop would shut up, would leave him alone.

"Well, that's just too bad, buster. I just now made up my mind that you're gonna come downtown and *testify,* see!" His voice was spiteful; it seemed he would make a big thing of the unimportant fight, just because of Berman's attitude of remoteness.

"Testify what?" Berman said flatly, pulling his eyes reluctantly from the sky.

"That you was here, that you saw everything. Like it or not, you *were* here. You saw it all—who hit who first, who started this. You was in the middle of it and you'll testify, just like anyone else."

Then Berman nodded almost humbly, suddenly affected by the policeman's fervor. He sighed a little for the ordeal, which had something pathetic, almost obscene about it. It was as though the policeman were requiring the motions of a lover from an old man long past that sort of thing.

"What's your name?" the policeman asked, flipping open his notebook and fumbling through his pockets for a pencil.

"Berman, Joseph Berman," he said in the thick, hot stillness of the street, with everyone watchful around him. A voice sounded from the distance, a woman's voice calling a dog or a child. A door slammed and its sound had something muffled about it, like sounds heard in a snowstorm. He could smell the sweat of the men around him.

The policeman eyed Berman suspiciously as he continued to search for the pencil. After all, some people *did* give the wrong name to avoid getting mixed up in things, and this poker-faced old Yid had tried to be "counted out."

"That's my name," Berman said wryly, figuring the look of skepticism on the policeman's face. Really it didn't seem right to Berman, though, applying that old name to what he was now.

The policeman grunted. He hadn't found the pencil and he looked wistfully toward his car parked a dozen feet away. Then he glanced around at all the people and figured they might try to elude him if he turned away, so he began again to search his pockets for the pencil.

And Berman looked around, too, as he waited. All the dim, moist faces of the onlookers, the other *witnesses*—to what? To themselves. . . . What strange creatures, always changing, growing, changing color and sound; exchanging their dreams like patrons of a vast library, into which they brought their old dreams for new, unused ones. But what happened to the old dreams? Berman thought he could see some of their markings on the dim, crowding faces. Here and there a crucifix glinted on a woman's breast, a medal on a man's dark chest. Dreams and flesh, imaginings and real smells and feelings. Love, too. What was it, something you could weigh or measure so that you could know the extent of your gains or your losses? No, a *dream*. And look at them all, full of those dreams, the dreams mixed with the smell of them, the smell and sound and sight of the whole staggering summer night.

The sky mantling its stars; the small movement of air he hadn't noticed until its ceasing. A holding of breath, cessation, everything waiting for another moment, a future without end, all built on the people's odd, gleaming, dream-dazed faces. The trees dead still, the sky low and heavy, and the small crowd caught in the silence around the policeman still grunting through his pockets, all breathing together in a little clump in the midst of the huge breathlessness of the night.

Then there came the faint hollow breath of distant thunder, just a massive suggestion at first. There was a dull, slow flicker of white light from far off.

"I felt a drop," the Italian fighter said.

His recent opponent, the Negro, just held one hand out, palm upward, testing.

Then all together, Berman with them, they looked up as though they could really hope to see the source of those startlingly cool pellets of water that tapped with increasing regularity on their hot faces.

"It's gonna come down all right," a woman said from the nearest steps.

Suddenly there was huge clap of thunder and the street was frozen in an instant's light. More thunder came and the rain fell harder. People began to run in different directions, the two fighters among them.

"Hey, you guys—come back here!" the policeman shouted. "Hey, all of you . . ." But his voice was tiny and insignificant and everyone had dissolved; there was no knowing where.

Only Berman remained, standing in the drumming rain beside the policeman. "You still going to want me for a witness?" he asked with a little smile.

The policeman just stared, bewildered, at the man before him, who stood calmly with the rain streaming off his hat brim, plastering his shirt to his great, ruined frame.

"Nah, go on, go on. Who the hell cares," the policeman growled, almost absently. Then he strode over to the car, slammed the door, and skidded off in a spray of water.

For a minute or two, Berman stayed there, all alone in the black downpour, the smile forgotten on his mouth. The water came cool and fierce on his face and body. He took off his limp hat and raised his face to the rain, mouth opened like a child's for the delicate taste. His lips moved, groped, as though to find each individual drop. He found himself trying, half-consciously, to recall that wondering note when the man had said, "I felt a drop." But so many drops, such conglomerate sensation. The rain fell on him, made runnings and miniature cascades over his features, down his neck, against his soaked shirt. He lost the source, no longer could tell the newly fallen rain from the secondary flows. His eyes were drowned in the torrent as he began to walk, and his step was slow and burdened with all of it as he sloshed through the sudden lakes and pools where the sewers were stopped up.

He felt an immeasurable relief, as if something that had been of great value, and pain, too, was removed from him, and he could dwell in the calm of contemplation. A little chuckle of self-ridicule escaped him. "I'm like a crazy kid out playing in the rain. I'll catch cold. . . . My Ruthie should see me." But he continued to walk at that unhurried pace, intermittently exposed in harsh light and shadow by the lightning, turning his head to look at houses and lighted windows, the dark, soaking foliage of the trees like heavy dresses weighted and dripping with rain, smelling through cleared nostrils the rain-softened ground and the crushed flowers.

He took off his glasses and carried them in his hand, for they were useless in the flooding rain. It gave his face a peculiar, naked look, a blind, almost terrible expression of trustfulness. Near his own street two women hurried by him. From under their umbrella they peered at him fearfully. He appeared awful and strange, walking so slowly, blindly, submissive and aimless in the downpour. Perhaps they thought he could be a despoiler; he seemed to have nothing to lose. Once past him their heels clacked more hurriedly.

He went into the emptiness of the house in a dazed yet matter-of-fact way. He took off his soaked clothes and toweled his body gently, without hatred. Then he dressed in clean, dry underwear. He went into the kitchen and made some hot tea, which he drank so quickly that his mouth was slightly sore and numb afterward.

Suddenly he wished to lie on his bed, as though he foresaw a marvelous aspect in rest after the long assault of the day. He turned off the kitchen light and went to his room. His bed groaned familiarly under him. A smile hovered just beneath a smile, didn't quite form; he was too eased even for that small positive expression. He just lay there, dry and cool in the dark room, watching the windows flicker and shimmer with the strange lights of the storm, listening to the rain drumming on the house until he drowsed.

After a little while he roused himself. He got up and went back into the kitchen, where he called his daughter. He spoke for only a few minutes, told her the one thing he knew would make her happy, then went back to bed. In a little while the rain put him into a really sound sleep and he never knew just when the rain stopped.

CHAPTER EIGHTEEN

All morning long he had avoided thought as he packed the last of his personal things in cartons, checked the closets and cellar for something he might have overlooked. Now the rooms were virtually bare and every move he made brought forth echo and reverberation.

His son-in-law had told him he would pick him up at four o'clock. It could be no more than two thirty now and everything was done. He glanced up toward the kitchen clock, but all there was to see was the clean disk where it had been, the one spot on the wall that seemed not to have aged with the rest. He went closer to look at the color that was so different from the rest, saw how strangely white it was, and tried to remember when the whole room had been that color.

He went into the bathroom and looked at himself in the mirror, running his hands over his jaw and chin. His color was a little gray; he still felt drained from the extraordinary journey through the heat the previous Saturday. He *could* shave, he thought. But the necessity of unpacking his razor and shaving cream from the neat, resigned carton changed his mind. Already he was in transit; he wanted no gestures of turning back. He sighed without sorrow.

189

"Ah, well," he murmured. And then he stopped to examine that habitual utterance, found himself suddenly eager to look into those little places in himself that he had always avoided. All right, he would stop that restless wandering around, that desperate searching for something to occupy himself with. Last week he had gone seeking something he wouldn't really have recognized if he found it. Or maybe he *had* found it? In any case, hadn't he been through the worst already? He had a little time. Well, let him use it to think, to ponder without anger or bitterness clouding his view. What was there to fear now? Was there anything at all?

He went into the living room, his heels thudding on the bare floors. There was nothing to recognize in his house. Where was the place in which he had lived? Was it possible that it was annihilated by time, that indeed it was now as though it had never existed?

He turned and went slowly back through the rooms, looking carefully, trying to answer that question first. The bathroom—Crane fixtures, the best. The girls' room, his own—empty, with only dust where the beds had been. In the room that had been his son's there was that faded enlargement of a boy in an A.Z.A. sweat shirt holding a fish aloft. It was the only thing in the room and he walked over to it, a little disturbed by the direct route he was able to take with all the furniture gone. He almost felt he should have edged in, gone the familiar route, pretending the furniture was still there. But no, no more ghosts. What was gone was gone. He marched almost boldly to the wall and stared at the picture of his son. From so close, the poor enlargement showed only a scattering, grainy texture joined in certain areas to darks and middle values. There was a suggestion of nose, a clotted shadow he knew to be eye. It was not his son. It was just a cheaply made monument, and he turned away from it in puzzlement, wondering whether there was anything left.

He went back to the living room and sat down on the one bridge chair still there. The rugs were rolled up against the wall under the window. He felt frail and old.

But there had been the maddeningly sweet taste of mead with raisins and plums in his mouth, there had been the haunting wail of a gull and the lowing of cattle, all together with the smells of bread and salt and mud and wine. . . . He raised that objection to the emptiness. And how come, then, that there had been the lined, beautiful face of his wife to fill him with passion, the awkward, soft incompleteness of his children to make him tremble with tenderness? And answer this, answer the heights he had dwelled on when he watched the river gliding in full flood yet without a ripple, without a sound, so that there was no way to see its movement. Was it nothing when he heard the river deep and soft going on and on without stop, and heard his father speaking above the roar, his father and God in one tumultuous voice with that living water?

Like a deaf man, he cupped his ear for some meaningful sound while the afternoon sunlight came in gently on the dust of his recent battleground.

And then, suddenly, he smiled, a weary smile, very remote from joy yet not bitter, either. He nodded his head, leaning forward on his elbows, and his expression was almost humorous, self-derogatory, as he began to speak aloud in the empty room, not disturbed by the talking to himself; for, as he reasoned, he wouldn't be alone any more, wouldn't be able to indulge that oddly satisfying eccentricity in his daughter's house.

"Go on, Berman," he said in a hoarseness that was almost a whisper. "Who you fooling? You knew all the time; inside you musta known what was out there in the dark. For a long time you knew it wasn't a God with a beard just out to get you. You knew that neither you or anyone else was made in His image. Face it and accept it, that as far as you can tell it *is* like nothing. Yes, it's a thing past what you can imagine, Yussel or Joe

or Berman or whatever you call yourself. Maybe, just maybe
. . ."

He had no words then for the thing he was sure of, sitting
in the dusty September sunlight on the one bridge chair remaining from all the appurtenances he had surrounded himself
with. But he phrased it in the hidden eloquence of his brain.
Answers come in little glimmers to your soul, most clearly in
childhood, in the sounds of certain voices and faces and things,
when you feel the miracle and the wonder; and he knew then
that the Torahs and prayer shawls and churches and saints were
just the art men tried to create to express the other, deeper
feeling.

"It's like a light that don't last long enough to recognize anything. But the light itself, just that you seen it . . . that's got to
be enough. . . ." And then more emphatically, almost desperately, for it was his last hope: "It *is* enough!"

Then he sat, feeling empty as an ancient, parched shell, yearning for the cool assurance of a trickle of sea water. He listened
for his son-in-law's car. There came to him the musical voices
of children coming home from school, a dog's bark, a plane's
engine far to the east. From the end of the street he heard a car
motor that could have been his son-in-law's. He stood up with a
small carton of belongings under his arm. He was ready.

"Ah, well," he conceded, as though to some irrefutable point
of logic. Then he sighed for the last time in the dusty, abandoned room.